T0266953

THE REST IS MEMORY

Heathcliff Redux

Sisters

The Double Life of Liliane

The House at Belle Fontaine

I Married You for Happiness

Woman of Rome: A Life of Elsa Morante

The News from Paraguay

Limbo, and Other Places I Have Lived

Siam, or the Woman Who Shot a Man

The Woman Who Walked on Water

*Interviewing Matisse or the
Woman Who Died Standing Up*

THE REST
IS MEMORY

—

A NOVEL

—

Lily Tuck

Liveright Publishing Corporation
A Division of W. W. Norton & Company
Independent Publishers Since 1923

Copyright © 2025 by Lily Tuck

For information about permission to reproduce selections from this book, write to Permissions, Liveright Publishing Corporation, a division of W. W. Norton & Company, Inc., 500 Fifth Avenue, New York, NY 10110

For information about special discounts for bulk purchases, please contact W. W. Norton Special Sales at specialsales@wwnorton.com or 800-233-4830

Manufacturing by Lakeside Book Company
Book design by Barbara M. Bachman
Production manager: Gwen Cullen

ISBN 978-1-324-09572-9

Liveright Publishing Corporation, 500 Fifth Avenue, New York, N.Y. 10110
www.wwnorton.com

W. W. Norton & Company Ltd., 15 Carlisle Street, London W1D 3BS

10 9 8 7 6 5 4 3 2 1

TO LEE

We look at the world once, in childhood.

The rest is memory.

—LOUISE GLÜCK, *Nostos*

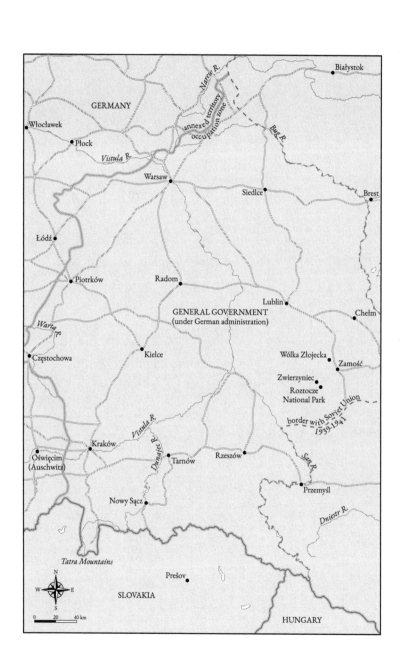

The NAME CZESŁAWA IS DERIVED FROM THE SLAVIC *ČA* which means to await and *slava* which means glory. What sort of glory awaits a fourteen-year-old girl—a gas chamber? a gunshot to the head? an injection of ten or fifteen milliliters of phenol directly into the heart?

Czesława is from Wólka Złojecka, a small village in southeast Poland. The nearest town to Wólka Złojecka is Zamość, founded in the sixteenth century by—and named after—Jan Zamoyski. Built by the Italian architect Bernardo Morando, Zamość is a perfect example of a Renaissance town.

On special feast days and occasions, Czesława and her family go to the Cathedral of the Resurrection of Our Lord and of St. Thomas the Apostle, also designed by Bernardo Morando, in Zamość.

Czesława is Catholic.

The time Czesława agrees to go to Zamość on the back of a boy's motorcycle, the boy, Anton—he is older, blond—warns her: "Don't tell your parents." Czesława does not tell her parents or how on the way back from Zamość—after they had each eaten a creamy *karpatka* Anton bought from a food stall in the market square—Anton stops the motorcycle by the side of the road and tells her to get off and unbutton the front of her dress. She does not. As he rides off on the motor-cycle, Anton shouts back at Czesława, "You owe me for the *karpatka*!" Although it has begun to rain, Czesława walks the six kilometers back to Wólka Złojecka.

Late for putting the chickens back in their pen, her father slaps her.

Czesława's father's name is Pawel.

Anton's secondhand motorcycle is made by Centraine Warsz-taty Samochodowe (Central Car Works). A Polish prewar company, Centraine Warsztaty Samochodowe manufactured motorcycles until the outbreak of World War II and the inva-sion of Poland. The invasion of Poland is sudden and quick and final. On September 27, 1939, the Poles capitulate to the Germans, after twenty-six days.

Pawel knows nothing about the invasion by the Germans— only that there are soldiers everywhere. Pawel has never once left Lublin Province. Each fall, he and his brother, Czesława's uncle, go to the Roztocze Forest—a part of the Zamoyski family estate—to poach for roe deer and red deer, taking him the farthest from the village of Wólka Złojecka Pawel has ever been.

One fall, in the Roztocze Forest, he shot a wild boar.

And, back home, in the evening, if there is company and after a glass or two of his homemade slivovitz, Pawel likes to tell stories about how he and his brother evaded and outsmarted the family game warden and, each time he tells of a narrow escape, he laughs loudly.

Haw haw!

The name slivovitz comes from *śliwka*, the Polish word for plum. Slivovitz is easy to make: the plums with their pits ferment in sugar, water, and grain alcohol. The area Czesława is from in southeast Poland is traditionally well-known for its slivovitz production. Each year, 100,000 tons of plums and prunes are grown in Poland.

In 1941, the German agrarian policy decreed: "God has helped us to conquer the Polish nation, which now must be destroyed; no Pole must have the right to own land or house. In ten years, the fields of Poland will be heavy with stacked wheat and rye raised and harvested by Germans, but not a Pole will remain."*

God made me out of nothing
    God made me because he loves me Czesława learns at her first communion catechism class. She also learns that the metal door set in the floor of one of the chapels in the Cathedral of the Resurrection of Our Lord and of St. Thomas the Apostle leads to the crypt where the Zamoyski fam-

---

*   Stanislaw Mikolajczyk, *The Rape of Poland, Pattern of Soviet Aggression* (New York: Whittlesey House/McGraw-Hill, 1948), 15.

ily is buried. The priest reads the inscription on the door: *Fundatoribus grata memoria*—In grateful memory to our benefactors.

"God made the members of the Zamoyski family," the priest says.

The priest is young, nervous. He has heard news of the German invasion.

"God loves them, too," he insists.

For Easter, Czesława and her mother always decorate eggs—an ancient tradition called *pisanki*. Eggs are plentiful, the family raises chickens.

For once, her mother is not busy cleaning, washing, cooking, milking, and she tells Czesława about her life as a young girl, a different sort of life, before she married Pawel.

Her mother's name is Katarzyna.

Katarzyna was once pretty, but mostly she is tired and too thin.

"How did you and Father meet?" Czesława always asks her.

Her mother does not answer.

With a metal pin, Czesława carefully makes a hole at each end of her egg, then, with the pin, she breaks the yolk inside—the part she is squeamish about: killing a chick embryo—and blows out the egg. Next, she applies melted wax with a special hollow stick to the shell before dipping the egg in various dyes, homemade from onion skins, berries, beets, and sunflower seeds. When the dyes dry, Czesława removes the wax.

———

Czesława's egg is red and green with a yellow flower design. To whom will she give the egg? To Anton? Thinking about him causes her to blush.

"What are you thinking about?" her mother asks. Her mother has a sixth sense.

When Katarzyna was Czesława's age, she fell in love with a boy—no, Tomasz was already a young man.

"I remember going to an air show in Blonia—a park outside of Kraków. I was thirteen or fourteen," Katarzyna says while they are decorating their eggs. "I still remember the dress I wore—a red dress." Katarzyna pauses and laughs. "One of the planes was an old biplane—a strange-looking contraption—and my father, who had worked at the Zieleniewski Machine Factory, built part of the engine and so of course he took us all to see the plane fly—me, my mother, my brothers, and my sister. I think my grandparents were there as well." Czesława's mother gives another laugh. "But to go on about the plane. Shortly after the plane took off—the plane was only a few feet off the ground—the engine exploded and the plane crashed to the ground, the wings breaking, and pieces of the plane scattering all over the field."

After a silence, Katarzyna also says, "One of these days I will take you to Kraków and show you where I lived. There is so much to see in Kraków—Wawel Castle, Jagiellonian University, St. Mary's Basilica—look how beautiful." Czesława's mother breaks off, holding up her own painted egg.

"One day, I would like to fly in an airplane," Czesława tells her mother, but her mother is not listening.

Her mother is busy putting the dyes and the decorating tools away.

"For next Easter," she says about the eggs.

Of all the chickens, Czesława's favorite is a pretty orange hen she named Kinga. Kinga lays delicate blue eggs that have a dark orange yolk.

A German soldier will wring Kinga's neck, pluck, cook, and eat her.

While they were in the Zamość market square eating their *karpatka*, Anton, his mouth full of cream, tells Czesława that he wants to be a pilot.

"You'll see," he tells Czesława. "Maybe one day, I'll take you for a ride in my airplane."

Anton laughs and, although Czesława does not believe him, she laughs with him.

Anton has a nice laugh.

Germany has 4093 bomber planes. Poland has 397 bomber planes—all but the twin-engine PZL.37 Łoś are obsolete.

Czesława and Katarzyna arrive at Auschwitz on December 13, 1942.

It is snowing on December 13, 1942.

Ever since she was a little girl, Czesława has the habit of open-ing her mouth and tilting her head back when it snows and letting the flakes melt in her mouth.

A cold drink from heaven.

Again, she opens her mouth to the snow when she is stand-ing in line at Auschwitz.

A guard yells at Czesława.

From 1941 to 1945, prisoner number 3444, Wilhelm Brasse, took more than forty thousand photographs of the men, women, and children interned at Auschwitz. A few minutes before he takes her photograph, Wilhelm Brasse, according to his memoir, sees the guard hit Czesława across the mouth.

> *Hesitantly, the girl came into the studio and sat in, or rather climbed on to, the revolving chair. She was like a frightened bird, and her haphazardly shaved hair gave her the look of a bald unborn chick. Brasse approached the seat.*
>
> *"What's your name?"*
>
> *"Czesława."*
>
> *"Are you Polish like me?"*
>
> *She nodded.*[*]

In the photograph, a bruise is visible just under Czesława's lower lip.

Photography was integral to the operation of some of the concentration camps. Whether taken for prisoners' identity papers, or as evidence of the most abhorrent medical experiments, photographs appear to have played an important role. For the official production of photographs, specialist departments were established, known as the Erkennungsdienst, or camp identification service. *

Born in Austria on December 3, 1917, to Rudolf and Helena Brasse (his father was Austrian and his mother was Polish), Wilhelm Brasse grew up in Zywiec, in south central Poland. He was working in his uncle's photo studio in Katowice, near the German border, when the Nazis invaded and he was arrested.†

On February 15, 1941, after he had spent six months at Auschwitz, Wilhelm Brasse is examined and interrogated about his photography and developing skills before he is

---

*   Janina Struk, *Photographing the Holocaust: Interpretations of the Evidence* (London: Routledge Taylor & Francis, 2020), 182.

†   Dennis Hevesi, "Wilhelm Brasse Dies at 94; Documented Nazis' Victims," *New York Times*, October 24, 2012.

ordered by a commanding officer to take the prisoners' pictures. He, the commanding officer explains, has two advantages over the other photographer candidates in the camp:

> *"The first is that you speak German, and I don't want to have to communicate with gestures, like a monkey. . . . The second advantage is that you—despite the fact that you insist on declaring yourself to be Polish—are the son and nephew of Austrians. It's my duty to pay special attention to Aryans. Even those who deny that status."**

As the camp photographer, Wilhelm Brasse will wear different, warmer clothes, he will eat better food, live in more decent conditions, and perhaps survive.

Czesława's prisoner number is 26947.
Katarzyna's prisoner number is 26946.

Of the 1057 Polish prisoners sent to Auschwitz from the Zamość region, between December 13, 1942, and February 5, 1943, whose names and fate have been established, 827 of them die. Most die within the first two or three months of their arrival at the camp.†

---

* Crippa and Onnis, *The Auschwitz Photographer*, 16.

† Helena Kubica, *The Extermination at KL Auschwitz of Poles Evicted*

Besides the chickens, Czesława's family owns a milk cow and a half-dozen pigs. The sow is huge. When she has her litter, she becomes aggressive and frightens Czesława. The story of a neighbor's child—a two-year-old girl—who fell into the pigpen and, before anyone could reach her, was devoured by a sow stays in Czesława's head. She hates those stories of gruesome deaths.

Czesława's mother, Katarzyna, milks the cow. She lets the milk stand and the next day she separates the cream from the milk. She churns the cream into butter and gives the buttermilk to the pigs.

"Here," Katarzyna tells Czesława, "take the bucket to the pigs. Don't fall in the pen," she adds with a little laugh.

Not funny, Czesława wants to say but does not.

There's also a dog. A brown-and-black crossbreed. The dog is a guard dog and not friendly. The dog lives outside the house, tied to a chain. The dog does not have a name. Czesława's father calls him—more likely he shouts at him—Pies ("dog" in Polish). He feeds the dog scraps and shouts at him some more.

Haw haw haw—in her head Czesława can hear her father's laughter.

The laugh makes shivers run up and down her back.

---

from the Zamość Region in the Years 1942–1943 (Oświęcim: Auschwitz-Birkenau Museum, 2006), 38.

———

*We were only ten feet away from the dumb-ass warden and he
could have smelled us.*

Haw haw haw.

Pawel is not tall but he is broad. He is missing the middle
finger on his left hand. An accident skinning the wild boar.
The stub has not healed properly and bleeds occasionally.
During dinner, Pawel wipes the nub on the tablecloth.

"Please, Pawel," Katarzyna starts to say to him.

"Leave me alone," he answers, pushing himself from the
table and knocking over the chair.

The dog's barking also makes Czesława anxious. The dog
barks all the time—at a cart on the road, the black crows in
the trees, a distant plane overhead.

"What happened to the pilot when the plane crashed?"
Czesława asks her mother while she is putting away the decorating tools for the Easter eggs.

"The pilot, a very handsome man named Tomasz—he
married one of my cousins and we went to the wedding in
Wadowice—survived. A miracle. But the strange thing,"
Czesława's mother continues, "is when I later mentioned the
plane accident to my sister, who is two years older than me,
she has no memory of it or of Tomasz. I know that memory is
unreliable, but I would swear on a dozen Bibles that the plane
crash took place. I also will never forget how Tomasz came

running across the field, waving his leather helmet in the air and shouting."

After a pause, Katarzyna says, "Then he ran straight up to me and took me in his arms and kissed me.

"I was wearing this red dress," her mother adds as if to explain.

In the summer of 1942, German soldiers round up Czesława's father, Czesława's uncle, and a dozen men from Wólka Złojecka and the neighboring villages. All of them are farmers who have tried to protest the confiscation of their land and animals first by the Russians, now by the Germans.

"My plow horses—a good team of bays—" Czesława's uncle complains. "Keret and—" He starts to name the horses before a soldier cuts him off.

The men are taken to the Roztocze Forest. This time, there is no joking or evasion on the part of Czesława's father and Czesława's uncle. Their hands tied behind their backs, they are shot and buried in a shallow mass grave.

For practice and for fun, the German soldiers shoot at some of the white storks that rise startled from their nests in the trees.

The storks, the Poles believe, bring good fortune.

After the men from Wólka Złojecka and the neighboring villages are rounded up by the German soldiers, Anton gets on his motorcycle and leaves as fast as he can for Russia. Along the way, he is stopped by a group of drunken Ukrainian peasants. The Ukrainian peasants beat Anton with their hoes and pitchforks and steal his motorcycle.

According to Hitler's instructions, preparations to expel Poles from their land and colonize it with German settlers begin in 1941. The first district to be selected where this deportation takes place is the Zamość region. The 110,000 inhabitants from 297 villages are to be divided into four groups: the first two groups are to be examined to determine whether they are suitable for germanization; the third group is to be sent to the Reich as slave labor; the fourth group is sent to Auschwitz.[*]

Czesława is in the fourth group.

The city of Zamość, also known as the "pearl" of the Renaissance, is renamed Himmlerstadt—Himmler Town.

The Zamoyski family, the richest aristocratic and politically important family of Poland, traces its roots back to the sixteenth century. One of its earliest and most famous family members, Jan Zamoyski (1542–1605), founded the second largest estate in the country (second only to that of the Radziwill family), which includes 23 towns and 816 villages and whose total area encompasses 17,500 square kilometers.

Notable Zamoyski family members—whose remains lie in the crypt of the Cathedral of the Resurrection of Our Lord and of St. Thomas the Apostle—are:

---

[*]   Kubica, *Extermination at KL Auschwitz of Poles*, 24.

JAN ZAMOYSKI (1542–1605), great crown
  chancellor and great crown commander
TOMASZ ZAMOYSKI (1594–1638), deputy
  chancellor of the crown
GRYZELDA KONSTANCJA ZAMOYSKA
  (1623–1672), mother of King Michał
  Korybut Wiśniowiecki
ANDRZEJ ZAMOYSKI (1716–1792), great crown
  chancellor, humanist, and reformer
WŁADYSŁAW STANISLAW ZAMOYSKI (1803–1868),
  politician, general, and activist
ANDRZEJ ARTUR ZAMOYSKI (1800–1874),
  political and economic activist
MAURYCY ZAMOYSKI (1871–1939), minister of
  foreign affairs of Poland
JAN TOMASZ ZAMOYSKI (1912–2002), Polish sena-
  tor and the last *ordynat* of the Zamość estate.*

For her First Holy Communion, in the Cathedral of the
Resurrection of Our Lord and of St. Thomas the Apostle,
Czesława wears a white dress and a myrtle wreath in her
hair. From her family, she receives a Bible with a white
leather cover. The date of her Holy Communion is inscribed
inside the Bible.

* "Zamoyski Family," Wikipedia, https://en.wikipedia.org/wiki/
Zamoyski_family, accessed December 22, 2023.

———

"The reason Saint Thomas the Apostle was referred to as the 'doubter,'" the young priest new to Zamość tries to explain to the children in his communion class, "is that, at first, he did not believe in the resurrection of Christ. But eight days after His crucifixion, Thomas sees Jesus and when Jesus bids Thomas to reach out his hand and thrust it inside His wound, Thomas finally believes in Him." While the young priest speaks, he makes the appropriate motion of thrusting his own hand into his side to emphasize Thomas's gesture.

The children watch the young priest but say nothing.

Later, at home, Czesława asks, "Was Jesus's wound still bleeding when Thomas reached in to touch it?"

In answer, Pawel only shrugs.

Czesława's grandmother hand-sews the white Holy Communion dress. She makes the lace around the collar and around the cuffs of the sleeves. Czesława's communion dress is much admired. The young priest new to Zamość, too, points to the lovely lacework, and says something complimentary to Czesława's grandmother who, in her confusion, takes the priest's hand and kisses it.

The young priest will also be murdered—gunned down in the street on his way to the Cathedral of the Resurrection of Our Lord and of St. Thomas the Apostle while leaning over to adjust the strap on his sandal. He is one of the 3000 members of the

Polish clergy to be killed by the Germans. Hitler's design for the repopulation of Poland did not include the Catholic Church.

The art of making lace was brought from Italy by Bona Sforza, who, in 1518, married King Sigismund I and became queen of Poland. She was intelligent, well educated, and spoke several languages. Besides lacemaking, Bona Sforza brought Italian culture and arts to Poland. She loved music, the theater, and dance. She also loved to eat and she introduced the Wawel Castle cook to cauliflower and tomatoes and to her favorite—pasta.

Two villages in Poland have kept up the tradition of lacemaking—Bobowa and Koniaków—and, each year, the village of Bobowa hosts a popular bobbin lace festival.

Authorized by Hitler, Heinrich Himmler oversaw a centralized concentration camp system that includes thirty to forty main camps and hundreds of smaller camps.

Turned into a "concentration village" during the war, Bobowa is one of those smaller camps.

No talk of lacemaking then.

As long as Czesława can remember, her grandmother, her father's mother, her *babciu,* has lived with them. Besides sewing and lacemaking, *babciu*—what everyone calls her—helps with some of the cooking and some of the washing, although Czesława's mother complains that *babciu* burns the oatmeal and the sheets are not rinsed out properly.

"I can't imagine marrying such an old man," making a face, Czesława once told her grandmother about Bona Sforza. "I learned about her in school. King Sigismund was fifty years old and Bona Sforza was only twenty-three. And she was hugely fat."

Czesława's school has been closed for two years—counting to 500 and writing one's own name, the Germans have decreed, is all Polish children need to know.

Her grandmother is illiterate and Czesława often reads aloud to her from one of her favorite books:

Make seven elephants, five camels, and three giraffes walk down the center of the main avenue. . . . And they're there. The humpbacked camels are plodding along, the solemn elephants are uncurling their trunks, and the giraffes are nodding their small heads on their long necks.

"Ha ha," Czesława laughs.

Kaytek, the hero of the novel, is a mischievous little boy who has magic powers. He can make people walk backward, he can change clocks, cause traffic jams. He creates havoc.

"Are you listening, *babciu*?" Czesława asks.

Her grandmother's eyes are shut, the lace on her lap has fallen to the floor, she is snoring.

Czesława reads on:

*Because as a grand finale Kaytek does one more spell. "Make the trees stand upside down."**

Czesława's grandmother slowly opens her eyes and says, "Go get your Bible, *kochanie*, and read me something nice."

Janusz Korczak, the author of *Kaytek the Wizard*, a hugely popular children's book published in 1933, was the director of a children's orphanage in Warsaw. He was a pediatrician and extremely brave. In 1942, he and the 196 Jewish children in the orphanage were sent to the Ghetto and from there to Treblinka, where they were exterminated.

A witness recorded seeing Janusz Korczak and the children leave:

All the children were ordered in groups of four, with Korczak at the head, with his eyes facing upwards, he held two children by their hands and led the march.

---

*   Janusz Korczak, *Kaytek the Wizard*, trans. Antonia Lloyd-Jones (New York: Penlight, 2012), 97, 99.

And when the German soldiers saw him, they asked: *"Who is this man?"**

Another witness, the poet Władysław Szlengel wrote:

> *Today I saw Janusz Korczak,*
> *As he walked with the children in the*
> *   last procession.*
> *And the children were in really clean clothes,*
> *As if they were going on a walk in the gardens on*
> *   Sunday . . .* †

One night, without warning or any indication of ill health, Czesława's grandmother, *babciu*, who is seventy-seven, dies in her sleep. She shares the room and the bed with Czesława. *Babciu* snores and keeps Czesława awake.

Her grandmother is the first dead person Czesława sees, but she is not the last. It is also the first and only time she sees her father cry.

But after drinking several glasses of slivovitz, Czesława's father no longer grieves for his mother and, instead, begins

---

* "Janusz Korczak—Biography," Muzeum Treblinka, https://muzeumtreblinka.eu/en/informacje/biography/, accessed December 22, 2023

† Gervase Vernon, "Dr. Janusz Korczak: Hero of the Warsaw Ghetto and Educator," *British Journal of General Practice*, 68 (October 2018): 485; doi 10.3399/bjgp18X699209, accessed December 22, 2023.

to rail against his life and his landlord, Jan Tomasz Zamoyski. Pawel complains about the ancient institution of entail—in Polish, *ordynacja*—that rules that the estate be inherited in full by the eldest son. Entail also decrees that the estate cannot be sold or mortgaged.

"My hands are tied," Pawel wails.

Babciu was fortunate is what later everyone says.

From their estate in Zwierzyniec, a city on the edge of the Roztocze Forest where the Germans have set up another deportation camp, Róża Zamoyska, the wife of Jan Tomasz Zamoyski, the last *ordynat* of the Zamość estate, has set up a nursery school and a hospital and saves 480 young children from being sent to extermination camps.

Róża Zamoyska is known as "the Angel of Kindness."

Róża Zamoyska is also known as "the Angel of Goodness."

In a photograph Róża Zamoyska is in her wedding dress, with one hand she is holding a large bouquet of flowers, with the other the arm of her husband, who is in uniform. They have been in love with each other for many years and they will go to Italy on their honeymoon. The year is 1938.

She is beautiful.

In another photograph, Róża Zamoyska stands with her husband. He has his arm in hers. She is wearing a coat with a large fur collar. They both look thin and tired but perhaps relieved. The photograph might have been taken at the end of the war. Next, their property will be confiscated and the Russians will imprison and torture Jan Tomasz Zamoyski. Róża Zamoyska will be forced to live elsewhere and work as a nurse.

She is still beautiful.

In a speech, Hitler said, "Our strength lies in our speed and our brutality. Genghis Khan hunted millions of women and children to their deaths, consciously and with a joyous heart. . . . I have put my Death's Head formations at the ready with the command to send man, woman and child of Polish descent and language to their deaths, pitilessly and remorselessly. Poland will be depopulated and settled with Germans."[*]

Czesława and her mother are given ten minutes to pack. They are each allowed a small suitcase and twenty zlotys (the equivalent of five dollars). Czesława has eight zlotys—money she has carefully saved.

Czesława packs the white leather Bible with the inscription of her First Communion date inside her suitcase. She packs a dress, a sweater, a few pairs of underwear, her nightgown, and the felt slippers she wears in the house.

Macht Schnell! Downstairs in the house, a soldier yells.

At the last minute as she leaves her bedroom, Czesława

* Richard J. Evans, *The Third Reich at War* (New York: Penguin Press, 2009), 27.

puts her jacks and the rubber ball in her coat pocket. She loves to play jacks and she is good at it. She can pick up all ten jacks at once. The trick is to throw the ball up high to have enough time.

The light blue cotton dress with a yellow zigzag pattern that buttons up the front that Czesława wears under her woolen coat is the same dress she wore when she rode on the back of Anton's motorcycle. Only then, it was a hot day in summer and not December. Since then, Czesława has grown and the dress is too small. It feels tight around her armpits and in her rush to get dressed a few of the buttons tore off. Never mind. The dress will be discarded and tossed on top of a mountain of used clothing.

So will her coat with the jacks and the rubber ball inside one of the pockets.

Downstairs a soldier again yells *Macht Schnell*!

Operation Himmler was the code name for the "false flag" operation and pretext used to invade Poland. Dressed in Polish uniforms, German soldiers partook in sham military skirmishes along the German and Polish border that implied Polish aggression and justified the start of World War II.

On December 10, 1942, in a long, slow line packed with horse wagons and carts, the evicted Poles are on their way to the transit camp in Zamość. At intervals along the way, armed soldiers in polished boots stand guard.

———

In a village a few kilometers from Wólka Złojecka, farmers who are about to be deported burn down their houses and barns, kill their cattle, pigs, horses, and poultry, rather than let the Germans settle on their property. Fifty-two people are shot in reprisal and buried in a mass grave.

In the crowded wagon on the way to the transit camp, Czesława reaches for her mother's hand.

"Have I told you the story of the Wawel Dragon?" Czesława's mother whispers to distract her.

"No" Czesława answers, although she has—many times.

"A very long time ago, a dragon terrorized a community by eating the sheep and all the local virgins. Then a man named Krakus came along and slew the dragon. The dragon became known as Smok Wawelski and Krakus became king and built the city of Kraków."

"Is this a true story?" Czesława asks.

Czesława will never get to Kraków; she will never visit Wawel Castle, Jagiellonian University, St. Mary's Basilica, or get to see where her mother grew up.

The Zamość transit camp is located in the poorest district of the city and in what was once the Jewish Ghetto. But all

the Jews in Zamość—7000 of them—are gone. They have
been either killed or sent to camps. When Czesława and her
mother, Katarzyna, arrive, they and the other detainees are
made to stand for hours in the market square. A woman nursing her baby attempts to sit down and is shot. Her husband
calls out and he is shot.

The purpose of the detention is selection. The Poles are
divided into groups and labeled:

> AA FOR those sent to Germany to do forced labor
> RD FOR those too old and infirm
> Ki FOR children under six whose features were
>   deemed "Aryan" and who would be germanized
> AG FOR those fit enough to be employed as laborers
>   by the German settlers
> KL FOR those to be sent to Auschwitz

During the three days Czesława and her mother are held in
Zamość, Czesława looks for Anton but does not see him in
the crowd of people—644 people.

Krystyna Trześniewska comes from the village of Majdan
Królewski. Majdan Królewski is 139 kilometers southwest
of the village of Wólka Złojecka. Both she and Czesława are
from the Polish province of Lublin and both are sent to the
Zamość transit camp on December 10, 1942.

———

When Krystyna, her father, Julian, and her mother arrive in Zamość, Krystyna's mother, also named Katarzyna, is nine months pregnant. She gives birth at the transit camp. The baby dies and Krystyna's mother is deported to a different town.

In Wilhelm Brasse's prisoner photograph of Krystyna, she has the same shorn head, the same little upturned nose as Czesława. She is wearing the same striped blue-and-gray uniform. Sixteen months younger than Czesława, Krystyna could be Czesława's sister.

Krystyna Trześniewska's prisoner number is 27129.

The other fourteen-year-old Polish girls from the province of Lublin, who arrive at Auschwitz on the same day as Czesława and Krystyna, are:

SALOMEA WĘSŁAWIK—prisoner number 27091

JADWIGA REPEĆ—prisoner number 27030

LUCYNA BIALEK—prisoner number 26831

IRENA LYŚ—prisoner number 26964

MICHALINA PIETRYNKO—prisoner number 27018

WACLAWA KROPORNICKA—prisoner number 26934

WANDA JAROSZ—prisoner number 26900

SALOMEA KOSTRUBALA—prisoner number 26932

WANDA BRONISLAWA OSIK—prisoner number 27002

HELENA PALCZYŃSKA—prisoner number 27023

HENRYKA ZALEWSKA—prisoner number 27110

SALOMEA FARFUS—prisoner number 27124

Lublin Province was one of the administrative regions of the interwar Second Polish Republic. The area was 26,555 square kilometers and the population was 2,116,200. According to the 1931 census, 85.1 percent of the population was Polish, 10.5 percent Jewish, and 3 percent Ukrainian.[*]

Ninety-five percent of Poles are Catholic.

After founding the beautiful Renaissance city of Zamość in 1588, the great crown chancellor, Jan Zamoyski, invited Jews, as well as Armenians, Hungarians, Greeks, Italians, and Scots to settle in the city. The Jews—mostly Sephardic Jews—were given equal rights, were exempt from paying taxes for twenty-five years, allowed to own houses, build a synagogue, a bathhouse, and a cemetery. They were also allowed to set up their own businesses—all but shoemaking, furriery, and pottery.

Krystyna's father, Julian Trześniewski, is a shoemaker.

On the train to Auschwitz, Czesława still looks for Anton but, again, she does not see him. The wagons are sealed and so

---

[*] "Lublin Voivoeship," Wikipedia, https://en.wikipedia.org/wiki/Lublin_Voivodeship, accessed December 18, 2023.

cramped there is no room for Czesława to sit. For three days, she stands. There is nothing to eat or drink—only what little people have brought with them. A bit of bread, a slice of cheese, some marmalade.

A woman offers Katarzyna and Czesława a slice of sausage. Czesława gags on it and cannot swallow the sausage. The woman scowls at her.

No one on the train knows where they are going.

"We are going to Germany to do forced labor," one man says.

"No, not to Germany, to Bełżec," another man says.

There are two small windows in their wagon and, at night while the train is moving, eleven people manage to climb out and escape. On another night, while the train is stopped in Kraków, three other people escape with the help of railway workers who, for a few minutes, unlock the car doors.

Pressed up against her mother and an old man who coughs and spits in her face, Czesława says, "I'm so thirsty."

"I know, I am, too," her mother answers.

"I have to go peepee," Czesława also tells her mother.

"Just pee in your underpants," her mother answers. "Everyone does."

The reason the men, women, and children from the Zamość region were sent to Auschwitz and not to Majdanek in Lublin, which was closer, was that, in 1942, Auschwitz is bigger—already it included Birkenau and had operational gas chambers—and could accommodate more prisoners.

———

Oświęcim, the Polish name for Auschwitz, was founded in 1270 and became an important salt and lead depot. The city's bridges over the Vistula and Sola Rivers provided one of the most traveled trade routes—on the one side, to Vienna and Kraków and, on the other, to Leipzig, Breslau, and Lemberg.

In 1655, Sweden invaded Poland, occupied Oświęcim, and burned the city down.

In 1804, Jakob Haberfeld, a Jewish distiller, founded a vodka and brandy factory that turned Oświęcim, rebuilt, into an agricultural station and a center for liquor production. Among his many different brands of vodka, the most popular were Zgoda, Czysta, Basztówka, Zamkowa, and Wiśniówka. Jakob Haberfeld also became one of the chief employers in a city where most of the population was Jewish.

In 1939, Alfons Haberfeld, the owner of the factory, and his wife, Felicja, went to the World's Fair in New York to exhibit their vodka and brandy at the Polish Pavilion. On their way home, the outbreak of World War II forced their ship to be diverted to Scotland and they were unable to return to German-occupied Poland.

While Alfons and Felicja Haberfeld were detained in Scotland, their five-year-old daughter, Franciszka Henryka, left behind at home in Poland, was sent to a death camp and died.

———

On arrival at Auschwitz, Czesława and her mother are taken to the bathhouse, where they are made to take off their clothes and strip naked. A guard rips out the opal earrings from Katarzyna's ears then shaves off all her body hair. It is the first time Czesława sees her mother naked and she looks away. Her mother is ugly and unrecognizable.

Czesława's long blond hair is cut off and her head is shaved. A guard laughs and says something in German Czesława does not understand as she shaves Czesława's few blond pubic hairs.

After a hot steam bath that scalds her flesh and a cold shower that freezes it, she is given striped blue-and-gray pants and shirt to match that are too large for her and a pair of wooden clogs.

Czesława is then tattooed on her left forearm.

"Forget your name," the guard tells her. "You are a number now."

26947.

It is also the first moment that fourteen-year-old Czesława realizes that all she knows may be useless.

The fact that Wilhelm Brasse, the camp photographer, spoke German was important since Polish was not allowed in the Erkennungsdienst, the camp identification service.

The Erkennungsdienst was located on the ground floor

of Block 26. There were two darkrooms, a room for loading cassettes, an office, and a room where the prisoners' identity photos were taken, which was furnished with a large-format camera and a revolving adjustable chair with a head support. A full front portrait, a three-quarter profile, and a profile photo were taken of each prisoner, then the prints were filed on 8-square-centimeter index cards with the prisoner's name, number, the date, the place of birth, and the place the prisoner was transferred from. The index cards were put into three separate groups: the living, the dead, and those who had been transferred.*

In Wilhelm Brasse's prisoner photograph, Katarzyna Kwoka, Czesława's mother, who is forty-six, looks much older. She looks shrunken and wizened.

"Don't keep touching it," Czesława's mother repeatedly tells Czesława about the bruise under her lower lip, "or it will get infected."

Their barrack, Block 13, is a breeding ground for lice, and rats proliferate. There is no water or place to wash. Czesława and her mother sleep on filthy straw mattresses on makeshift wooden bunks. The latrines are outside and foul.

Helena Rycyk is the youngest female prisoner in the camp. She is six. Her prisoner number is 27032. Helena's mother,

* Struk, *Photographing the Holocaust*, 103–4.

Feliksa, tries to keep Helena's nine-year-old brother, Tadeusz, in the women's camp, by dressing him as a girl. This subterfuge works for a few days and Tadeusz is given a number from the women's general series: 27033. A few days later, however, his true gender is revealed and Tadeusz is taken away to the men's camp. He is given a new prisoner number, 83910.

Helena and Tadeusz are from the village of Sitaniec. Sitaniec is four kilometers north of Zamość and on the road that leads to Wólka Złojecka. Sitaniec is where Czesława's elementary school was. And how many times, she wonders, have she and her family driven past Sitaniec on their way to shop in Zamość or to go to mass at the Cathedral of the Resurrection of Our Lord and of St. Thomas the Apostle? The village of Sitaniec—or after they had driven past it—is also where Anton stopped his motorcycle and told Czesława to get off and unbutton her dress.

Tadeusz and his older brother, Stanislaw, are murdered by lethal phenol injections.

The head of the SS disinfection commando at Auschwitz, Josef Klehr, devised an inexpensive way to speed up the killing process. An injection of ten or fifteen milliliters of phenol directly into the heart causes death within fifteen to twenty seconds.

The victim is brought in and seated on a footstool; his left arm is raised sideways and his chest is thrust out to make his heart more accessible to the lethal injection. Sometimes the victim is blindfolded.

Of the approximately 160 children under eighteen from the Zamość region sent to Auschwitz, half were boys. Forty of the boys were under fifteen. Of the forty boys, seven survived the camp.*

Of the fourteen-year-old girls arriving at Auschwitz from the Zamość region on December 13, 1942, six survive.

In October 1940, Poland was divided between Russia and Germany. The Soviet zone was integrated into Russia while the Germans integrated Pomerania, Silesia, and Posnania into the Reich. The center and rest of Poland was named Generalgouvernment and was ruled by the Germans. The concept of Poland, Hitler announced, would be erased from the human mind.

The Zamość area was declared "the First Resettlement Area" of the Generalgouvernment.

While standing at the Zamość transit camp waiting for selection, Czesława saw a girl she knew. Jadwiga Repeć was in

*   https://anchor.fm/auschwitz-memorial/episodes/On-Auschwitz
-26-Deportations-of-Poles-from-the-Zamo-region-to-Auschwitz
-elsov31.

THE REST IS MEMORY

Czesława's communion class. Jadwiga is also from the village of Sitaniec and one time, Pawel, Czesława's father, gave her a ride home in the cart. Czesława was tempted to wave to Jadwiga and she nudged Katarzyna, her mother, who was standing next to her.

"Look, I know that girl," she whispers.

"Sshh," her mother whispers back.

"She was in—" Czesława starts to say.

"Sshh," her mother whispers again, "or they will shoot us."

Jadwiga Repeć's prisoner number is 27030.

Jadwiga had admired Czesława's white Holy Communion dress—the lace, in particular—and Czesława said something polite in return about Jadwiga's dress. It was a lie and she felt the weight of it on that day. Would she have to confess it to the young priest?

"I saw you on the back of Anton's motorcycle," Jadwiga tells Czesława, when she has the chance to speak to her. "I saw you twice. On your way to Zamość and on your way back from Zamość," she says with a laugh.

"That was not me," Czesława answers Jadwiga. "And I don't know any Anton," she adds.

Two more lies.

At Auschwitz, in their crowded barrack, Czesława tries to avoid Jadwiga.

Czesława's mother, Katarzyna, tries to remember how she knows Jadwiga's mother but at the moment cannot.

"Anna Repeć," she repeats softly to herself.

Instead, unbidden, comes the memory of Tomasz, the handsome pilot, who kissed her when she was very young. At her cousin's wedding, although he did not appear to recognize her, something about Tomasz still caught Katarzyna's whole attention—her heart, she thinks. From then on, she physically compared every man she met with Tomasz. None match him—not Pawel.

Katarzyna wanted to go to university, she wanted to be a teacher; instead she milks cows, churns cream into butter, feeds chickens, cooks, washes, irons, and, in summer, helps Pawel work in the fields. Fields that do not belong to them.

Established on July 8, 1589, the Zamoyski family entail was one of the largest in Europe. By 1939, before the invasion of Poland, the estate consisted of five hundred thousand acres of farmland and forest that included villages, sawmills, paper mills, breweries, sugar refineries, several palaces, valuable paintings, and a library of illuminated manuscripts and books. Six years later, on February 21, 1945, the Zamoyski family entail ceased to exist. The Russian Communist government took over the estate, divided it between over a thousand families, and introduced agricultural reforms.

The entail is a form of trust, established by deed or settlement, that restricts the sale or inheritance of an estate in

*real property and prevents the property from being sold,
devised by will, or otherwise alienated by the tenant-in-
possession, and instead causes it to pass automatically,
by operation of law, to an heir determined by the settlement deed.* *

When drunk on slivovitz, Pawel always railed loudly on his
perceived injustices.

"Even these plums are not mine," he yelled, gesticulating,
and spilling the liquor in his glass.

In September 1939, the Russians occupied the Zamoyski
estate, then, a month later, the Germans took control of the
estate. Fortunately, Jan Tomasz Zamoyski was allowed to
continue to administer it under German supervision from his
property in Zwierzyniec.

Zwierzyniec, a city at the edge of the Roztocze Forest, was
also turned into a transit camp. Between 20,000 and 24,000
Poles were processed there, many of them children—those
who looked Aryan were forcibly taken from their parents and
sent to Germany for adoption.

"Tadeusz made a cute little girl," Czesława tells Krystyna.

"He could have fooled me," Krystyna answers.

* "Fee Tail," Wikipedia, https://en.wikipedia.org/wiki/Fee_tail#
Polish-Lithuanian_Commonwealth, accessed December 18, 2023.

———

Little Helena Rycyk dies at Auschwitz on December 10, 1943.

Sitting cross-legged together on the dirty straw mattress, Czesława and Krystyna eat their ration of soup and bread and exchange stories.

Her mouth full, Czesława quotes, *"Make seven elephants, five camels, and three giraffes walk down the center of the main avenue."* She has read *Kaytek the Wizard* so many times she knows parts of the novel by heart.

*"Make the roses in the garland change into wieners and the mandolin into a big sausage,"** Krystyna quotes right back. She, too, knows parts of the novel by heart.

The two girls forget where they are for a few seconds and laugh.

"Don't refuse a child if he asks you to tell the same story over and over and over again," Janusz Korczak, the author of *Kaytek the Wizard*, advises.[†]

"I had a cat, a gray cat, called Kala," Krystyna also tells Czesława. "She slept on my bed. She purred so loudly she sometimes woke me up," Krystyna says. "I miss her."

---

*   Korczak, *Kaytek the Wizard*, 97.

†   Janusz Korczak, *Ghetto Diary* (New Haven: Yale University Press, 2003), 32.

"I had a chicken," Czesława tells Krystyna.

"Pock-pock," she says, but does not laugh.

One spring, on his own initiative, Wilhelm Brasse took a photograph of a small bunch of violets growing on the grounds of Auschwitz. He retouched and colored the print and affixed it to the wall of his studio. Instead of being blamed or punished for taking the photograph, Brasse was praised for it. The print of the bunch of violets was much admired and copied. The copies were made into postcards and the German guards sent them back home to their families.

Souvenir from Auschwitz.

Czesława and her mother and a dozen women in the barrack are put to work clearing a pond. They have to gather silt into wheelbarrows and push the heavy wheelbarrows up a steep embankment. The cold handles stick to their hands. Their feet in the wooden clogs ache. It is freezing and the ground is slippery.

Guards, stamping their leather boots and holding dogs on leashes, shout at them.

"Don't fall," Katarzyna warns Czesława, "or they'll set the dogs on you."

Czesława often wonders about Pies, their guard dog—the dog who did not have a name and was chained outside their house in Wólka Złojecka. Although she did not like the dog— she was afraid of him—she often dreams about him. In one of the dreams, she is walking through a field of wheat and the dog is following her. The dog is friendly and when she speaks to him, the dog wags his tail. Another thing that she remarks about the dog is that his eyes are different colors. One eye is blue and the other eye is brown. In the dream, Czesława thinks that this is a sign of good luck and she wishes she had had time to free Pies.

One of infamous Dr. Mengele's studies involved experimenting with people whose eyes are of a different color, a condition known as *heterochromia iridum*. He also experiments with injecting chemicals into the eyes of living subjects in the attempt to change the color of their eyes.

Early one cold and dark morning, Czesława and her mother and the women from the barrack are driven from their beds and made to stand outside for a roll call.

"What do you think happened to the dog?" Czesława asks her mother.

"Sshhh," her mother says.

"Do you think the dog is dead?"

"Sshhh," her mother says again.

The women stand facing the barbed-wire fence that imprisons them. A bright light from one of the sentry towers shines on the barbed-wire fence, which is electrified, and on a woman who is hanging from it.

"Yes, the dog is dead," Czesława's mother answers when they are finally allowed to return to the barrack.

———

"Do you know what today is?" Czesława's mother also asks.

Czesława shakes her head.

"Christmas day."

Strings of lights decorate the roofs of several barracks and the Auschwitz orchestra plays while a woman with a high voice repeatedly sings *"Stille Nacht, heilige Nacht. Alles schläft, einsam wacht."* Throughout the night, the guards celebrate and shoot their pistols at random.

"Did you know her?" Czesława asks her mother.

"Who?" Czesława's mother asks.

"The woman on the fence—the barbed-wire fence," Czesława answers.

"We talked a few times. Her job was cleaning the latrines. Poor woman," Czesława's mother says.

"A Jew," she adds, making the sign of the cross.

"Don't forget to say your prayers," Katarzyna also tells Czesława.

> *Hail Mary,*
> *Full of Grace,*
> *The Lord is with you.*

On her knees in front of the bunk, Czesława dutifully prays with her eyes shut.

———

Dr. Hans Frank, Hitler's lawyer and responsible for the shipment of thousands of Poles as slave laborers, became the administrative head of the Generalgouvernement, as occupied Poland was known. Dr. Frank's headquarters is in Kraków and he and his wife, Brigitte Herbst, live in Wawel Castle.

Brigitte Herbst rides around the Kraków Ghetto in an open Mercedes, calling herself the "queen of Poland." She buys jewels and furs from the Jews, intimidating and threatening them. There is a photograph of her dressed in a white ermine coat. She is a despicable human being.

Dr. Frank spends as much time as he can in Zwierzyniec at a hunting lodge next to the Roztocze Forest. The hunting lodge has been transformed into a German officers' club and is filled with elite Nazi officials. From the hunting lodge, Dr. Frank and the Nazi officials go out into the forest and shoot pheasants.

Later they will eat pheasant schnitzel in a beurre blanc sauce and drink a lot of red spätburgunder wine.

Czesława thinks about her hen, Kinga.

What would she do for just a single egg?

"For breakfast, I had porridge with milk," Czesława tells Krystyna. "Then for lunch I had borscht, bacon and—"

"For lunch I had fried fatback and sauerkraut," Krystyna interrupts Czesława.

"For dinner, I had potato soup and bread," Czesława continues.

"I wonder where my mother is," Krystyna says.

To eradicate Polish culture, the Germans shut down the schools and universities, seized the press, confiscated the art in museums, burned the archives, and removed all the monuments and statues to Polish heroes. Already in 1939, they had murdered 6000 intellectuals, professors, magistrates, lawyers, physicians, and clergymen.

A list of Polish writers who perished during World War II:

JÓZEF CZECHOWICZ died in the bombardment of
    Lublin on September 9, 1939
STANIZLAW IGNACY WITKIEWICZ committed
    suicide one day after the Red Army invaded
    Poland, on September 18, 1939
TADEUSZ DOŁĘGA-MOSTOWICZ was killed by
    Soviet soldiers on September 20, 1939
WŁADYSŁAW SEBYŁA died in the mass executions
    known as the Katyń Massacre on April 11, 1940
    (22,000 Polish officers were killed)
STANISŁAW PIASECKI was executed in the
    Palmiry Forest on June 12, 1941 (from 1939 to
    1941, German police killed 1700 Polish civilians
    in the Palmiry Forest)

TADEUSZ BOY-ŻELEŃSKI was killed in a mass
execution in Lviv, known as the Massacre of
Lviv Professors, on July 4, 1941

HERSEHELE DANIELEVICH died of hunger in the
Warsaw Ghetto in 1941

OSTAP ORTWIN was murdered by a Gestapo
officer for refusing to wear the Star of David in
the spring of 1942

DEBORA VOGEL was murdered (along with her
husband and son) during the liquidation of the
Lviv Ghetto in August 1942

JANUSZ KORCZAK was murdered along with the
children of his Warsaw orphanage in Treblinka
on either the fifth or sixth of August 1942

BRUNO SCHULZ was murdered in Drohobych in
November 1942

WŁADYSŁAW SZLENGEL died during the Warsaw
Ghetto Uprising on May 8, 1943

ZYGMUNT RUMEL was killed in the massacre of the
Polish population in Volhynia on July 10, 1943

ANDRZEJ TRZEBIŃSKI, active in the resistance
movement, was executed in Warsaw on
November 12, 1943

EDWARD SZYMAŃSKI died at Auschwitz on
December 15, 1943

ZUZANNA GINCZANKA was killed in Kraków by
the Gestapo in 1944

KRZYSZTOF KAMIL BACZYŃSKI was shot by a
German sniper during the Warsaw Uprising on
August 4, 1944

JULIUSZ KADEN-BANDROWSKI was killed
by a shell during the Warsaw Uprising on
August 6, 1944

TADEUSZ GAJCY, along with his fellow poet
ZDZISŁAW STROIŃSKI, died during the
Warsaw Uprising on August 16, 1944

KAROL IRZYKOWSKI died of a blood infection,
after being wounded during the Warsaw
Uprising, on August 2, 1944[*]

Except for Janusz Korczak, the author of *Kaytek the Wizard*,
Czesława has never heard of or read any of these Polish writers.

On August 4, 1942, a day before he and his orphaned children
are marched off to the trains bound for Treblinka, Janusz
Korczak wrote in his *Ghetto Diary*:

> *I am watering the flowers. My bald head in the window.*
> *What a splendid target.*

---

[*] Mikołaj Gliński, "Death and Survival in WW II: A Polish Writer's Perspective," *Culture.pl*, September 18, 2014, https://culture.pl/en/article/death-survival-in-wwii-a-polish-writers-perspective, accessed December 18, 2023.

He has a rifle. Why is he standing and looking on calmly?

He has no orders to shoot.

And perhaps he was a village teacher in civilian life, or a notary, a street sweeper in Leipzig, a waiter in Cologne?

What would he do if I nodded to him?

Waved my hand in a friendly gesture?

Perhaps he doesn't even know that things are—as they are?

He may have arrived only yesterday, from far away. . . . *

"Do you remember how Kaytek is turned into a dog at the end of the book?" Czesława asks Krystyna. "He has hurt one of his paws and is dragging along on three legs, complaining how hard a dog's life is and how dependent a dog is on the kindness of people for food and a home."

Again, Czesława wishes she had turned Pies loose.

Jan Tomasz Zamoyski and his wife, Róża Zamoyska, would certainly have heard of and read a few of those Polish writers.

Of the 110,000 Poles evicted from their villages in the Zamość area between February 1942 and August 1943, 30,000 were children. Of those 30,000, an estimated 4454 children between the ages of two and fourteen, who were considered "racially

---

* Korczak, *Ghetto Diary*, 115.

valuable," were selected for germanization. The rest were sent to either labor camps or concentration camps.[*]

As soon as Róża Zamoyska got permission from Odilo Globocnik, Lublin's district governor, to establish a nursery in Zwierzyniec, she embraced the children who had been imprisoned in the camp as if they were hers—she would have five of her own. Each morning, she got up before dawn, lit the fire in the kitchen, boiled milk, put the milk into bottles, then drove to the camp to feed the children.

"This morning, a woman who was holding two small children in her arms couldn't keep up with the others. She was so thin and frail. When I ran over to help her a guard knocked me down with his rifle," Róża tells her husband. "Don't worry, I am fine," she also tells him. "I got up right away and went up to another guard who let the woman and her children go free. A small victory," she adds with a smile.[†]

Anna Repeć is a tall angular-looking woman. At the Sunday market in Sitaniec, she and Katarzyna had once had an argument over the price of butter.

"Your butter tastes peculiar," Anna Repeć accused Katarzyna.

---

[*]   Roman Hrabar, Zofia Tokarz and Jacek E. Wilçzur, *The Fate of Polish Children During the Last War* (Warsaw: Interpress, 1981), 132.

[†]   https://sp3szczebrzeszyn.edupage.org/text/?eqa=dGV4dD10ZXh 0L2Fib3V0JnNlYnBhZ2U9MQ%3D%3D.

"It's spring. It's normal. The cows eat onion grass," Katarzyna answered her.

The reason, perhaps, Katarzyna did not want to remember where she met Anna Repeć.

Anna's body is covered with a painful red rash and dark scabs, the result of typhus. During roll calls and on her way to work, she does her best to hide her skin's condition so that she won't be selected unfit for work.

On March 23, 1943, Anna Repeć will be sent to the death block and gassed.

A long time ago—or what seems like a long time ago to Czesława—she had had an itchy and painful rash on her arms and chest. When she showed the rash to her mother, Katarzyna handed her a bucket and told Czesława to go to the pasture and wait for the cow to pee.

"Eww, that is disgusting!" Czesława had protested as her mother sponged the cow's urine on first her arms, then her chest.

"Sit still and don't be silly," her mother had answered.

"It smells horrible."

"You'll see the rash will be gone by tomorrow."

The single latrine is outside. It can only be used at certain times during the day. The women have to stand in line waiting their turn to go in. They all have dysentery. Unable to wash, their clothes are soiled with excrement.

———

Occasionally while she works clearing out the frozen mud from the pond, Czesława hears planes flying overhead and she wishes she could look up and wave to them. If she did, a guard would beat her.

"Hello, Anton," she waves to him in her head.

"Hello, Czesława," Anton answers as he circles the plane and comes back for her.

Marianna Rycaj is also from the village of Wólka Złojecka. She and Katarzyna know each other well and are old friends. In summer, they share the vegetables from their kitchen gardens.

"All those cucumbers I planted," Katarzyna tells Marianna. "We pickled a bunch of them last summer. I wonder what happened to all those jars," she asks.

Marianna shrugs and says, "The Germans probably ate them."

"We should have put poison in the jars," Katarzyna says.

Marianna nods but does not smile.

Marianna Rycaj's prisoner number is 27038 and, in Wilhelm Brasse's photograph, she has an honest, plain face. She is familiar with the medicinal properties of and uses for local herbs and plants. People come to Marianna from all over the

Zamość region—from the villages of Sitaniec, Wysokie, Bortatycze, Zarudzie, Krzak, and Złojec—to cure their boils, their backaches, their coughs, their sprains. They pay her with what they have—a bag of potatoes, a side of bacon, a quart of milk, a basket of apples.

Marianna Rycaj tells Katarzyna Kwoka about the curative properties of cows' urine.

One Easter, Katarzyna gives Marianna a pretty painted egg.

Pawel always makes fun of Marianna Rycaj. He says she is old and ugly. He also says that she is a fraud—her remedies are useless. The time he cut off his finger with a knife while he was skinning the wild boar, the bitter tea she prescribed did not help. It made things worse; he was up all night vomiting.

At Auschwitz, Marianna's thirteen-year-old son, Mieczyslaw, dies from a lethal phenol injection to the heart.

On his way home from school, Mieczyslaw Rycaj would sometimes stop in front of Czesława's house and tease the chained dog.

"Ha ha, you can't get me, ha ha."

And, just out of the dog's reach, Mieczyslaw would jump up and down and flap his arms.

"Ha ha, try and get me," Mieczyslaw yelled at the dog again.

Driven into a frenzy, the dog barked and lunged in vain at Mieczyslaw.

One day Mieczyslaw threw an apple at the dog.

Sitting cross-legged on the dirt floor of their barrack, Czesława and Krystyna play a makeshift game of jacks with pebbles they have found and hidden in the pockets of their striped blue-and-gray uniforms. A larger pebble substitutes for the rubber ball.

"Throw it up high," Czesława instructs Krystyna.

"Like this," she shows.

Before she throws the larger pebble up in the air, Krystyna crosses herself and laughs.

"I wish I could see my father. Just for a minute," Krystyna tells Czesława. "I know he is here. We arrived together, but we were separated."

"For my thirteenth birthday, he made me a beautiful pair of red leather shoes," Krystyna also says before she begins to cry.

The name of both Czesława and Krystyna's mothers is the same: Katarzyna. For some unspoken reason neither Czesława nor Krystyna mentions this.

Although he fought against them as a lieutenant in the Polish Cavalry in 1939, Jan Tomasz Zamoyski is allowed to administer the Zamoyski estate so that he can provide food for the occupying German army. Managing the estate also allows him to get involved in many clandestine activities to help his countrymen. He belongs to the Union of Armed Struggle and the Home Army and, under his code name Florian, he collects funds and ammunition for the underground and finds hiding places for resistance fighters, Allied prisoners, and downed airmen in the Roztocze Forest. A forest that Jan Tomasz says he knows as well as he knows the back of his hand. An elegant hand he extends.

The last time Pawel went to the Roztocze Forest, he did not come back. Perhaps, Katarzyna thinks, it was a form of retribution. A retribution for all his unlawful animal slayings. Poor Pawel. She prefers not to think about him lying in an unmarked mass grave. Also, if she is honest, his memory is fading. She can barely remember what Pawel looked like— his hair, the color of his eyes. As for his lovemaking—she gives a harsh little laugh—there was little love there.

One June, Katarzyna had seen a muster of white storks feeding in the freshly plowed earth of their fields—at least fifty of them. When Pawel chased them off, they had spread their great black and white wings and soared into the air, clacking their beaks, sounding like gunfire.

"Promise me," Katarzyna had turned to Pawel then and said, "that one day you will take me to the Roztocze Forest to see the storks' nests."

"Sure, I promise," Pawel had answered. In spite of his scorn for women, Pawel was a bit in awe of Katarzyna—her city upbringing, her book learning.

———

The Germans burn down the Zamoyski Family Library on Marszałkowska Street in Warsaw. Of the 120,000 rare books and manuscripts in the library only 1800 survive the fire. Many of them are saved from further destruction by Jan Tomasz Zamoyski, who packs the books and manuscripts into cases and brings them to the Pauline Monastery in Jasna Góra for safekeeping.

At night, during the first few weeks in camp, Katarzyna gets on her knees in front of her bunk covered with filthy straw and prays:

> *Hail Mary, full of grace,*
> *the Lord is with you,*
> *blessed are you among women. . . .*

She makes Czesława get on her knees and pray next to her.

"Pray to the Virgin Mary, Queen of Poland," Katarzyna tells Czesława. "She won't forsake us."

Instead, Czesława thinks about the young priest—what was his name? Father . . .

After a few weeks, Katarzyna prays alone on her knees. After a month, too tired and worn out, Katarzyna stops praying on her knees.

The tomb slab of Jan Zamoyski, the founder of Zamość, rests on the floor of the Zamoyski family chapel in the Cathedral of the Resurrection of Our Lord and of St. Thomas the Apostle.

Portraits of Zamoyski family descendants line the walls of the
chapel. A metal door next to the chapel entrance leads down
into the Zamoyski crypt. *Fundatoribus grata memoria* is how
the inscription on the crypt door reads.

In school, Katarzyna learned enough Latin to translate the
words for herself: In grateful memory to our benefactors.

"Benefactors," Katarzyna repeats to herself. "I wonder
where they are now?"

Of the 1301 Polish men, women, and children who were in
the first three transports from the Zamość transit camp to
Auschwitz, only 230 known prisoners survived. The old,
the sick, the infirm, the unfortunate who attracted a guard's
attention—and who is shot—were immediately herded on to
trucks and sent to the gas chambers and were never counted.[*]

In Tadeusz Borowski's short story "This Way for the
Gas, Ladies and Gentlemen," the narrator, a prisoner at
Auschwitz—like the author—describes the unloading of a
transport train:

> *Here is a woman—she walks quickly, but tries to appear*
> *calm. A small child with a pink cherub's face runs after her*
> *and, unable to keep up, stretches out his little arms and*
> *cries: "Mama! Mama!"*
>
> *"Pick up your child, woman!"*

[*]   Kubica, *Extermination at KL Auschwitz of Poles*, 38.

"It's not mine, sir, not mine!" she shouts hysterically and runs on, covering her face with her hands. She wants to hide, she wants to reach those who will not ride the trucks, those who will go on foot, those who will stay alive. She is young, healthy, good-looking, she wants to live.

But the child runs after her, wailing loudly: "Mama, mama, don't leave me!"

"It's not mine, not mine, no!"

Andrei, a sailor from Sevastopol, grabs hold of her. His eyes are glassy from vodka and the heat. With one powerful blow he knocks her off her feet, then, as she falls, takes her by the hair and pulls her up again. His face twitches with rage.

"Ah, you bloody Jewess! So you're running from your own child! I'll show you, you whore!" His huge hand chokes her, he lifts her in the air and heaves her on to the truck like a heavy sack of grain.

"Here! And take this with you, bitch!" and he throws the child at her feet.

"Gut gemacht, good work. That's the way to deal with degenerate mothers," says the S.S. man standing at the foot of the truck. "Gut, gut, Russki."*

---

* Tadeusz Borowski, "This Way for the Gas, Ladies and Gentlemen," in *This Way for the Gas, Ladies and Gentlemen*, trans. Barbara Vedder (New York: Penguin Books, 1976), 43.

———

"Why is it that nobody cries out, nobody spits in their faces, nobody jumps at their throats?" The writer Tadeusz Borowski asks in another story that is in the form of a letter to his fiancée, Maria, who like him is a prisoner at Auschwitz, and then answers: *"Our only strength is our great number—the gas chambers cannot accommodate all of us."**

When Jan Tomasz Zamoyski walked into the office of General Odilo Globocnik to try to persuade him to release the children from the Zwierzyniec internment camp, a huge Alsatian dog jumped him. Then General Globocnik shouted at Jan Tomasz: "So you have come here to oppose the orders of the police and SS, who are to impose order on recalcitrant scoundrels and conduct huge purges to liquidate 'Die Polnische Banditen,' and you expect me to help you with this?"

Odilo Globocnik, the Lublin district governor and police chief in charge of expelling Poles from their houses and lands, proposed the use of gas chambers in concentration camps to exterminate the Jews more rapidly and efficiently. For his cruelty and ruthlessness, Odilo Globocnick was known as "the devil's accomplice."

* Borowski, "Auschwitz, Our Home (A Letter)," in *This Way for the Gas*, 112–13.

Standing there in front of Globocnik, it was clear to Jan
Tomasz that if he was not careful, he could easily end up in
Lublin Castle prison or, worse, at Auschwitz. Putting forward
the strongest argument he could think of, Jan Tomasz replied
that he would never interfere in police matters and that he had
only come because he did not believe that the Great German
Reich could be waging a war on children and that he was con-
vinced it could show magnanimity toward those tiny individu-
als who were innocent yet had to suffer because of their elders.

In the end, after being further questioned about the
facilities available for the children in Zwierzyniec, Jan
Tomasz was at last relieved to hear that General Globocnik had agreed to his proposal, which he called an
"extraordinary favour."

The first thing a relieved Jan Tomasz Zamoyski did when
he left General Globocnik's office was drink a large glass of
vodka. Then he wrote Róża, his wife, that he had managed to
persuade Globocnik to release all the children under six years
of age in the Zwierzyniec internment camp.*

Czesława was tempted to tell her mother about Mieczyslaw
teasing the dog and her mother, she believed, would tell

---

*   Kubica, "Account of Jan Zamoyski, a Witness of the Evictions in the
Zamość Region, on the Saving of Evicted Children from the Camp for
Poles in Zwierzyniec," in *Extermination at KL Auschwitz of Poles*, 260–61.

Marianna Rycaj, Mieczysla's mother, and Mieczyslaw will be punished.

Only she didn't and now it is too late.

"What do you think happened to the dog?" Czesława asks her mother again.

"Sshh," her mother answers.

They are lying next to each other in a bunk on the filthy straw.

"Stop worrying about the dog and go to sleep," her mother says.

For a reason she cannot explain Czesława keeps thinking about the dog—a dog with no name.

"Don't forget to say your prayers," her mother says.

During the German occupation, the Polish Catholic Church was in disorder. The Germans killed several thousand priests. In Rome, Pope Pius XII offered little support, instead advocating compromise with Germany. The Polish primate, Cardinal Hlond, had left Poland and had taken refuge in a Benedictine abbey in Savoy, France, and did not offer spiritual aid to his parishioners. Instead, in a 1936 pastoral letter, Cardinal Hlond wrote condemning the Jews: *"It is a fact that Jews are waging war against the Catholic Church, that they are steeped in free-thinking, and constitute the vanguard of atheism, the Bolshevik movement, and revolutionary activity. It is a fact that Jews have a corruptive influence on morals and that their publishing houses are spreading pornography.*

It is true that Jews are perpetrating fraud, practicing usury, and dealing in prostitution."

Cardinal Hlond continued his letter with *"It is good to prefer your own kind when shopping, to avoid Jewish shops and Jewish stalls in the marketplace."**

Pawel heard about the first deportations of Jews from Zamość on April 11, 1942, and how the entire Jewish population had been herded into the market square. Some of the Jews had been shot on the spot.

Everyone in the village of Wólka Złojecka knew about it but few spoke about it.

"Three thousand Jews were sent to Bełżec," Pawel's brother told him, shrugging.

"There were too many of them," Pawel answered.

In 1941, the 7000 Jews in Zamość had been forced to move to a ghetto.

Pawel then started to complain to his brother about a transaction on Hrubieszowska Street in Zamość over the purchase of a new axle for his plow in which he felt he had been grossly overcharged.

"You wouldn't believe how those people live," he added.

Sometimes Czesława's mother talks in her sleep.

---

* Ronald Modras, *The Catholic Church and Antisemitism: Poland, 1933–1939* (London: Routledge, 1994), 346.

"Tomasz!" Katarzyna calls out. "Tomasz!"

"Who is Tomasz?" in the morning, Czesława asks her mother.

"Is Tomasz the pilot who survived the plane crash?" Czesława, remembering, also asks.

Her mother shrugs.

Barely alive after his beating, Anton joins the 1.7 million Poles deported by the Russians to Siberia for forced labor, and is sent to a lumber camp near the Arctic Circle. In the six-month-long winter, the temperature in the camp ranges from minus 2 degrees to minus 36 degrees Fahrenheit.

At Auschwitz, the barrack Czesława and her mother are in was once a stable. It was divided into eighteen stalls for fifty-two horses. There are no windows, only a row of skylights overhead. A chimney duct that runs the length of the barrack supplies a bit of heat in winter. The three-tier wooden bunk beds that are installed in the stalls should, in theory, accommodate the same number of people as it did horses, but, in 1942, 400 women live in the barrack.

In a middle wooden bunk, Czesława sleeps next to her mother and Katarzyna sleeps next to Krystyna and Krystyna sleeps next to Ewa, who is from the village of Złojec, and Ewa sleeps next to a woman who dies.

Ewa snores and reminds Czesława of her grandmother, *babciu*.

Krystyna cries for her mother in her sleep.

Katarzyna calls out to Tomasz in her sleep.

Czesława worries about the rats she hears scurrying across the wooden floor and she cannot sleep. She tries to pray but the words of her prayer have gone missing.

On Sundays, when the weather was fine, Pawel, Katarzyna, and Czesława walked the three kilometers from Wólka Złojecka to the village of Złojec. The Church of Christ the King is wooden and small and more intimate than the Cathedral of the Resurrection of Our Lord and of St. Thomas the Apostle in Zamość. Her prayers, Czesława liked to think, can reach God more easily from Złojec.

"Is *babciu* in heaven now?" Czesława asks her mother.

"Yes, I am sure she is," her mother answers.

"And is *tata* in heaven, too?" Czesława asks about her father, Pawel.

Katarzyna does not answer.

Czesława's grandmother spoke both Polish and Russian. When she was a child, Polish was forbidden in the schools. Schoolchildren, too, had to speak Russian among themselves otherwise they were punished.

"Punished how, *babciu*?" Czesława asks.

"Beaten."

"Priests, too, were beaten," Czesława's grandmother continues. "And all the convents and monasteries were shut down. The worst was that the Catholic liturgy had to be said in Russian."

"Did you pray in Russian?"

"The signs on the shops—the butcher, the bakery, even the shop where I bought my thread—had to be in Russian. The reason I never learned how to read," Czesława's grandmother says. "It got so bad that it was a crime to baptize children with Polish Christian names—can you imagine?"

Czesława shakes her head.

"It was a terrible time," Czesława's grandmother says.

"The Russians are terrible people," she also says.

"I bought the cotton thread for the lace in Nowa Osada—the poorest district of Zamość, where all the Jews lived," Czesława's grandmother goes on. "The shop was in a squalid basement on Ogrodowa Street and the owner only spoke Yiddish and although I did not understand him, he was friendly and he did not overcharge me for the thread."

Czesława nods but she has never been to Ogrodowa Street. She does not know what Jews are nor does she ask.

The first deportation of the 7000 Jews from the Zamość Ghetto began on April 11, 1942, during Passover. 3000 Jews were transported in cattle cars to Bełżec.

The second deportation occurred at the end of May, during Shavuot, and Jews were sent to Sobibór.

The third deportation of Jews was on August 11, 1942. 300 to 350 Jews were transported to Majdanek.

The fourth deportation was in September and 400 Jews were sent to Bełżec.

The fifth and final deportation, which marked the end of the Zamość Ghetto, was in mid-October. 4000 Jews were sent to Bełżec and to Sobibór.*

"I remember the last time I went to buy thread on Ogrodowa Street," Czesława's grandmother also says. "It was an extremely hot day and when I arrived at the basement shop, I thought I was going to faint. The Jewish shop keeper brought me a cold drink. The drink was a little bitter but also sweet—hard to describe it. I had never tasted anything like it before and right away I felt better. When I tried to ask the shop keeper what the drink was made of—an herb, I assumed—he did not understand me. Funny, I still think about that drink and wonder what it was made of."

"Marianna Rycaj might know. She knows all about herbs and remedies," Czesława tells her grandmother.

But her grandmother is not listening to her and goes on, "The Jewish man was very kind. Not like the Russians."

On March 5, 1940, Stalin signed an order for the execution of 22,000 Polish military officers and intellectual prisoners that became known as the Katyń Massacre—named for the forest where, years later, the mass graves were discovered. General Vasili M. Blokhin, chief executioner for the NKVD (People's Commissariat of Internal Affairs, the Soviet secret police)

* https://www.belzec.eu/media/files/pages/240/zamosc_ang.pdf.

personally shot 7000 of the Polish officers during twenty-eight consecutive nights in the Russian city of Kalinin.

Blokhin had each prisoner brought into a small prison basement room painted red—known as the Leninist room—for identification, then the prisoner was led to another room with padded walls and a drain on the sloping concrete floor. The prisoner's hands were tied behind his back and he was placed against a wall. Dressed in a rubber apron and wearing leather gloves, Blokhin entered the room and, using his own German-made Walther pistol (he distrusted the standard-issue Soviet arm), shot the prisoner in the head. His plan was to work for ten hours nonstop and shoot 200 prisoners each night—an average of one prisoner every three minutes.

As a reward, Blokhin received the Order of the Red Banner from Joseph Stalin.[*]

Among the Poles who died in the Katyń massacre were an admiral, 2 generals, 24 colonels, 79 lieutenant colonels, 258 majors, 654 captains, 17 naval captains, 85 privates, 3420 non-commissioned officers, 7 chaplains, and 200 pilots.[†]

The 146 Polish pilots who managed to escape to England and fought in the Battle of Britain were much commended. They

[*]   "Vasily Blokhin," Wikipedia, https://en.wikipedia.org/wiki/Vasily_Blokhin, accessed December 18, 2023.

[†]   "Katyn Massacre," Wikipedia, https://en.wikipedia.org/wiki/Katyn_massacre, accessed December 18, 2023.

were aggressive and courageous. Often reckless, they flew dangerously close to the enemy. They achieved a remarkable score of 203 enemy planes destroyed, 35 probables, and 36 damaged. The 303rd Polish Fighter Squadron, one of the sixteen Polish squadrons in the Royal Air Force (RAF) during World War II, had the highest kill ratio and was the most successful Allied squadron shooting down German aircraft.*

When Krystyna asks Czesława if she has ever had a boyfriend, Czesława hesitates. She is tempted to invent a whole romance for herself—Anton slowly unbuttoning her dress and kissing her—and lie.

"No," she finally answers.

"Have you?" she asks Krystyna.

Father Wojciech, Czesława remembers all of a sudden—the young priest.

In the lumber camp close to the Arctic Circle, Anton has lost two of his toes to frostbite.

In late summer, the Roztocze Forest was a dense green and deeply familiar. Pawel knew every path, glade, and tree. When he looked up, he could see the storks' nests and he guessed that the chicks had hatched and were gone and that the storks,

---

* Marius Gasior, "The Polish Pilots Who Flew in the Battle of Britain," Imperial War Museum, https://www.iwm.org.uk/history/the-polish -pilots-who-flew-in-the-battle-of-britain, accessed February 2, 2024.

too, would soon leave for their winter home in North Africa. Although the German soldiers had tied his hands behind his back and he was being marched along with his brother and the men from Wólka Złojecka and the neighboring villages, Pawel still hoped he might survive.

He did survive for a few seconds. The bullet only grazed the back of Pawel's head. He fell to the ground and, lying among the dead men, he shut his eyes and held his breath. Pawel never saw the soldier who walked over to him and shot him in the head again.

At first, Ewa, the woman from the village of Złojec who is lying next to the woman who died, thought the woman was sleeping.

"Roll call," she whispers to her. "You better get up."

Ewa nudges the woman. "Roll call. Get up," she says more loudly.

Afraid all of a sudden, Ewa calls out to Czesława's mother, Katarzyna, "She won't wake up."

"Quick, take her shoes," Katarzyna tells Czesława about the dead woman. "They are better than yours."

On arrival at Auschwitz, Czesława had to give up her little suitcase, which she had packed with her Bible with the white leather cover and with a few clothes. She also had to hand over the clothes she was wearing—her coat with the jacks and rubber ball in the pockets, her blue dress with the yellow zigzag pattern, her underwear, socks, and her one good pair of brown leather shoes.

"You'll get them back," a guard had assured her.

Czesława's brown leather shoes along with Krystyna's new red leather ones are lost in a mountain of 100,000 pairs of shoes.

When Wilhelm Brasse, the Auschwitz prisoner photographer, was liberated in 1945 and had returned to Zywiec, his home-town in Poland, he tried to resume his photography business but couldn't. "When I tried to photograph young girls, for example, dressed normally," he said, "all I'd see would be these Jewish children."[*]

Years later, Wilhelm Brasse still pictures Czesława sitting in the chair about to be photographed, looking like a little fright-ened bird. When he asked her if she was a Pole like him, he could barely hear her answer—she was.

Not only the Jewish children, he thinks.

During roll call while it is sleeting and so cold it is difficult to stand still or stand at all, the commandant of the camp, Rudolf Höss, who is wearing a thick leather coat, a fur-lined hat, and woolen gloves, stops by to inspect them. Commandant Höss holds his little long-haired dachshund on a leash. He picks up the dog in his arms and nestles the dog against his face,

---

[*] Hevesi, "Wilhelm Brasse Dies at 94."

saying: *Mein Liebling, mein kleiner Liebling.* He whispers the dachshund's name—Schatzie.

Commandant Höss goes and stands in front of one of the girls and stares at her for a moment. She is young and still healthy and he motions her to leave the group and follow him.

The girl hesitates.

"Come," Commandant Höss says, walking up to her.

"What's your name?" he also says.

"Salomea," the girl whispers.

"A beautiful name for a beautiful young girl," Commandant Höss says, taking Salomea by the arm.

Commandant Höss has two daughters, Heidetraud and Inge-Brigitt. Inge-Brigitt Höss is nine years old. She is unaware that a concentration camp with thousands of prisoners exists fifty yards from her well-appointed two-story villa—a villa filled with art and furniture stolen from the Jewish prisoners—that she shares with her father and mother, her sister, and her two brothers and where she has lived for three and a half years. In the villa's pretty walled-in garden, there is a fun slide and she plays games with her sister and brothers. From her upstairs bedroom window Inge-Brigitt can see a crematorium tower but pays it no mind unless the wind blows in the wrong direction and billows of black smoke come her way. One time, her sister, Heidetraud, who is a year older than Inge-Brigitt, complaining about the smell, says: "I wonder what in God's name they are burning?"*

---

*   Thomas Harding, "Heaven in Auschwitz: Living as a Killer's

THE REST IS MEMORY

———

At first the bodies of the prisoners were buried in mass graves but soon the numbers became too great and crematoriums were introduced. The first crematorium was built by the Erfurt firm of Topf and Sons and installed at Auschwitz in 1940:

> *the furnace was 50 per cent more powerful than the Dachau model of 1939 . . . [and] estimated an output of 30 to 36 in 10 hours, or about 70 bodies for a 20-hour cycle. . . . on August 15 everything [was] ready, and the first cremation was carried out satisfactorily in what became known as Auschwitz crematorium I.*[*]

A few months later a second furnace is needed; less than a year later a third.

"It's filled with evil, and this evil is narrated with a disturbing bureaucratic obtuseness; it has no literary quality, and reading it is agony," writes Primo Levi in his introduction to the autobiography of Rudolf Höss. *"Furthermore, despite his efforts at defending himself, the author comes across as what he is: a coarse,*

Daughter," *The Independent*, September 8, 2013.

[*] Yisrael Gutman and Michael Berenbaum, *Anatomy of the Auschwitz Death Camp* (Bloomington: Indiana University Press/United States Holocaust Memorial Museum, 1998), 189–90.

*stupid, arrogant, long-winded scoundrel, who sometimes bla-
tantly lies.*

*"In a climate quite different from the one he happened to grow
up in, Rudolph Hoess [sic],"* Levi continues, *"would quite likely
have wound up as some sort of drab functionary, committed to dis-
cipline and dedicated to order—at most a careerist with modest
ambitions. Instead, he evolved, step by step, into one of the great-
est criminals in history."**

"He is the nicest *papi* in the world," Inge-Brigitt says about
her father, Rudolf Höss, "and I love Schatzie. I love all dogs,"
she adds.

Valentin Oblomijev, one of the guards assigned to the infamous Hundestaffel (Dog Handler Company) at Auschwitz,
takes pleasure in frightening prisoners by letting loose his
dog, a German shepherd, on them as they arrive off the
trains and as he escorts them to the gas chambers. The
children are especially afraid of the dogs. The dogs can
easily knock them to the ground and rip out their throats.†

* Primo Levi, introduction to *Commandant of Auschwitz, The Autobiography of Rudolf Hoess*, by Rudolf Hoess, trans. by Constantine FitzGib-
bon (London: Weidenfeld & Nicolson, 2000), 19.

† "SS-Wehrpass from an Auschwitz Dog-Handler," Alexander Historical
Auctions, Lot 572, October 28, 2020, https://www.alexautographs.com/
auction-lot/ss-wehrpass-from-an-auschwitz-dog-handler_00144D1971,
accessed December 18, 2023.

———

On his way from the train to the camp, Mieczyslaw Rycaj keeps as far away from the dogs as he can.

Troubled about what happened to the dog chained outside their house, Czesława still dreams about him. The dreams make no sense. In one, the dog is female and has huge swollen pink nipples. The dog, a bitch, is nursing her pups. When, in the dream, Czesława leans down and tries to pick up one of the pups, the dog bites her.

"Bring me a rope!" Pawel shouts to Czesława, one spring afternoon a few months before he is taken away and shot in the Roztocze Forest.

Alone in her room—her mother and grandmother have not yet returned from shopping in Zamość—Czesława is playing jacks. Her first thought is that her father knows she is playing jacks instead of doing housework. He is going to use the rope on her. Pawel has a temper.

"Quick, a rope," Pawel shouts again. "I'm in the barn."

Her head tied to a rail, the cow stands in a stall shifting her weight and bellowing. Two small yellow hooves protrude from her distended vagina.

Without a word, Pawel takes the rope from Czesława and ties the rope around the little hooves. His hands are bloody.

"Hold up her tail," Pawel tells Czesława.

Czesława watches as he pulls at the hooves and as the cow struggles and kicks out at Pawel.

"Hold her tail, I said," Pawel says again, then swears as the cow defecates on his hands.

Pawel pulls on the rope and little by little the calf's black legs emerge.

"Is he going to live?" Czesława asks.

Pawel doesn't answer.

Streams of mucous-like blood cling to the legs and spatter against Czesława's arm and she shuts her eyes.

She can hear Pawel grunting and swearing as she holds up the cow's tail and as she keeps her eyes closed.

"There," she at last hears Pawel say and Czesława opens her eyes.

A shapeless black mass half covered with a whitish membrane emerges from the cow's vagina and, without a word, Pawel lets it drop to the ground.

The calf is dead.

Pawel swears again and goes to untie the cow and wash his hands.

Back in her room, Czesława picks up the jacks but, instead of playing, she begins to cry. She wishes her mother was there and she could tell her about the calf. But when her mother comes home, Czesława says nothing.

Pawel also says nothing.

Instead, he says, "You're late, Katarzyna. Where is dinner? I'm hungry."

———

A pregnant prisoner at Auschwitz does not survive long. She is either given a phenol injection or, if her pregnancy is advanced, a forced abortion. Should she give birth, her baby is right away drowned in a bucket of water.

For dinner, the prisoners receive a bowl of soup made from rotten vegetables, a piece of stale bread, a small piece of cheese.

Holding up her piece of stale bread, Czesława says, "Make my bread into a potato."

Holding up her piece of stale bread, Krystyna says, "Make my bread into an apple."

Holding up her piece of stale bread again, Czesława says, "Make my bread into a *karpatka*."

"Do dogs dream?" Czesława asks her mother, who is lying next to her in the crowded bunk.

"Sshh," her mother says, "go to sleep."

"Maybe the dog is dreaming about me," Czesława says.

"Sshh," her mother says again. "Don't talk nonsense."

"Don't look at her," a woman prisoner whispers to Czesława as they walk back from clearing the pond of silt. With her head, the woman motions to a guard who is standing at the gate.

"If anyone dares to look at her, she sends them straight to the gas chamber."

Maria Mandl was the SS-Lagerführerin of the women's camp at Auschwitz and responsible for the death of half a million women and children. She was brutal, violent, and sadistic.

"I saw her tear a child from its mother's arms and when the mother tried to intervene, she beat the woman to the ground. She then kicked the woman in the mouth repeatedly and so hard that all the woman's teeth fell out."

"She is known as *the Beast*," the same prisoner whispers.

"They far surpassed their male equivalents in toughness, squalor, vindictiveness, and depravity." Rudolf Höss wrote in his autobiography—an autobiography he wrote while he was awaiting his trial—about the female guards. *"Most were prostitutes with many convictions, and some were really repulsive creatures. Needless to say, these dreadful women gave full vent to their evil desires on the prisoners under them, which was unavoidable. . . . They were soulless and had no feelings whatsoever."**

Maria Mandl was convicted of crimes against humanity and sentenced to death in Kraków's Montelupich prison. On January 24, 1948, at age thirty-six, she was hanged.

Rudolph Höss was tried for murder and hanged on April 16, 1947. He was hanged on a short-drop gallows, by the same

---

*   Hoess, *Commandant of Auschwitz*, 135.

method and on the exact same site in Auschwitz that was once used to execute prisoners.

Montelupich was a Nazi prison where an estimated 50,000 political prisoners were tortured and killed during World War II. After the war, Montelupich became a Soviet prison where, in turn, Polish soldiers were tortured and killed.

Tomasz, Katarzyna's handsome pilot who survived the plane crash, is one of the 50,000 political prisoners who is killed in Montelupich prison.

"In Kraków," Katarzyna tells Czesława, "I lived on Szlak Street near the Jalu Kurek Park, where I would go after school. The park was once the garden of the Montelupi family. The street their house was on was named after them. So was the prison. I wonder what happened to Tomasz and whether he is still alive," she adds.

"Tomasz, the pilot?" Czesława asks again.

At Auschwitz, some of the other female prison guards are: Margot Drexler, Therese Brandl, Irma Grese, Elisabeth Ruppert, Elisabeth Saretzki, and Gertrude Zloros.[*]

"Poor Jadwiga," Czesława whispers to Krystyna.

"Did you see? Her eye was covered with blood."

[*] Gutman and Berenbaum, *Anatomy of the Auschwitz Death Camp*, 396.

"A guard hit her in the face with a club. One of those women."

"Jadwiga sat down while she was digging the ditch for the latrines. She was sick."

"Poor Jadwiga," Czesława says again.

Twice a day, the women in Czesława's barrack are allowed to squat for a few minutes on a wooden plank placed on top of a ditch in order to relieve themselves. They all suffer from diarrhea or worse, dysentery. They cannot wipe or properly clean themselves. Their garments are soiled. They stink.

There is no drainage, no sewage treatment plant for the latrines, and the women's excrement flows untreated into the Vistula and Sola Rivers. Auschwitz is located at the confluence of the two rivers.

"I fell in love with Tomasz when I was thirteen. A man who fell from the sky," Katarzyna whispers to Czesława. "A man who kissed me."

Czesława does not answer. She does not know what to say.

"Can you imagine such a strange thing," Katarzyna continues, "a young girl falling in love with a grown man she has only seen once—oh, yes, she saw him again a few years later at his wedding but that only made her love for him that much stronger—he was so handsome—and can you imagine, Czesława," Katarzyna repeats, "that this child, now a grown woman, kept right on thinking about him every minute of the day and part of every night, too, for the rest of her life? And the man does not know that she is in love with him or even know that she exists. And if he did, he might not care." Katarzyna pauses for a moment.

Katarzyna's talk about her undying love for Tomasz confuses and upsets Czesława. Katarzyna sounds like a stranger.

What about Pawel? She wants to ask her mother but does not dare.

"And the grown woman," Katarzyna goes on, "who is married and has a daughter and lives on a farm and works hard is still thinking about this man and imagining romantic episodes with him—he is kissing her, he is making love to her—" Katarzyna breaks off. She has a fever, her body is burning and covered with an itchy rash, lice are eating her up.

"It's a silly story," she says. "It's a fairy tale."

Czesława is tempted to tell her mother about Anton—Anton unbuttoning her dress and kissing her—but does not.

And to distract her mother, she whispers, "Tell me again how Kraków got its name—the story of Krakus and the dragon."

Katarzyna is silent.

"Please, tell me about Krakus," Czesława says again, more insistent.

"Oh, Krakus," Katarzyna says, rousing herself. "Krakus had a beautiful daughter named Wanda and after Krakus

died, Wanda ruled Poland. A German king wanted to marry
Wanda and when she refused him, he invaded Poland."

"Who was the German king?" Czesława interrupts.

"His name was Rytygier and when he was killed in battle
Wanda committed suicide."

"Did she love Rytygier?" Czesława says.

"There are two versions of the story," Katarzyna answers.
"The first is that Wanda committed suicide as a sacrifice to the
gods for her victory in battle. In the second version, Wanda
committed suicide because she knew there would always be
suitors who wanted to marry her and her refusal would pro-
voke them to wage war. Wanda wanted to prevent that."

"Which version do you believe?" Czesława asks
her mother.

After a pause, and instead of answering, Katarzyna says,
"Wanda committed suicide by throwing herself into the
Vistula River."

Jadwiga loses an eye.

Distraught, Jadwiga's mother, Anna Repeć, offers Jadwiga her daily rations of 300 grams of stale bread, her bowl
of rotten turnip soup, her moldy piece of cheese, but Jadwiga
refuses the food.

In the morning, during roll call, Jadwiga does not get
up. She lies curled up in a fetal position on a bunk bed inside
the barrack. Later when Jadwiga's mother leaves for work,
Jadwiga has not moved from the bunk bed. In the evening

when Anna Repeć returns to the barrack, her daughter, Jadwiga, is gone.

"Did you see her eye?" Krystyna asks Czesława.

Czesława nods but says nothing.

"My uncle lost an eye," Krystyna continues. "He was hammering and the nail flew out and hit him in the eye. He got a glass eye, but the glass eye did not fit properly and he kept taking it out. It was gross."

Czesława should have told Jadwiga the truth: she did ride twice through the village of Sitaniec on the back of Anton's motorcycle—once on her way to Zamość and once on her way back from Zamość.

Not to think about Jadwiga, Czesława asks Krystyna, "Do you want to play a game of jacks?"

Along with the instructions, a note inside the box Czesława's jacks came in said that in Ancient Egypt, children played jacks with sheep bones.

On their way to Zamość, Czesława and Anton ride by the Sitaniec cemetery and Anton lets go of one of the handlebars to point at something—a gravestone.

"Careful," Czesława says into his back.

"My *babciu* is buried there," he shouts as he speeds up the motorcycle.

The Centraine Warsztaty Samochodowe (Central Car Works), the Polish company that manufactured motorcycles, was partially nationalized and renamed Państwowe Zakłady Inżynieryine (State Engineering Works—PZInż for short). During the war, the factories were confiscated and dismantled and the engineers were either killed or sent to Germany as slave laborers.

The women from the village of Sitaniec, who were evicted from the Zamość region and sent to Auschwitz on December 13, 1942, gather around Anna Repeć to comfort her. They are:

AGNEISZKA FLACZ—prisoner number 26864

ANNA PROC—prisoner number 27019

WANDA WRÓBEL—prisoner number 27100

KATARZYNA KOSSOWSKA—prisoner
   number 26904

ELŻBIETA SAŁAMACHA—prisoner number 27055

KAROLINA SAŁAMACHA—prisoner number 27057

JANINA DZIECKAN—prisoner number 26852

FELIKSA RYCYK—prisoner number 27031

FRANCISZKA KAPLON—prisoner number 26915

ANNA KAPLAN—prisoner number 26930

ANNA PUZIO—prisoner number 27010

Most of the women were once good-looking, healthy, loved, and bedded. Most of the women, except for Karolina

Sałamacha and her older sister, Elżbieta Sałamacha, who never married, had husbands who are either missing or dead. Most of them were sturdy farmworkers who plowed and sowed fields, milked cows, made butter, fed chickens, cooked, and cleaned. Most of them bore children who are also either missing or dead. All of them went to mass every Sunday and prayed on their knees. And all, but Feliksa Rycyk, who will be evacuated to Bergen-Belsen and from there liberated, suffer from severe malnutrition and are sick with dysentery and typhus. Within three months of their arrival at Auschwitz, all eleven women—including Anna Repeć—are gassed.

Feliksa Rycyk, the sole female survivor from the village of Sitaniec, testified at a court hearing in Zamość, on June 12, 1946:

During the eviction of Sitaniec on December 6th, 1942, at the same time as all the other Poles, my entire family, i.e. my husband, our three children, and I, was driven out by SS-men, They put us in a camp in Zamość . . . [then] they took my family, myself, and many others to Auschwitz. At Auschwitz our family was divided. . . . The two children I took remained with me until I contracted dysentery. That was when they took my son away and I was left with only my daughter . . . she died of neurosis of the heart and the measles. What happened to my sons, I do not know. They told me that when Tadeusz fell ill and died, they burned his body. The other son was called Stanislaw and he was *older. . . . The number 27031 is tattooed on my arm. In the camp there were very many people evicted from the Zamość region, but very few returned.**

Along with their excrement, the ashes of the murdered prisoners are dumped into the Vistula and Sola Rivers.

"Do you know how to swim?" Czesława asks Krystyna.

"No. Why do you ask?" Krystyna answers.

"I don't know," Czesława answers. She doesn't.

"Last summer, I went to a lake in the Roztocze Forest," Krystyna says. "My father was going to teach me how to swim but it was raining."

"Did you wear a bathing suit?" Czesława asks.

"It was wool. And scratchy," Krystyna adds and laughs.

"Did you see the storks?" Czesława asks Krystyna. "My father said they come every year to nest in the forest."

"No," Krystyna says, shaking her head. "By late summer the storks are gone."

Year after year, in the spring, the storks return to the same nests where they mate and give birth. Some of the nests are very old. In the village of Kościerzyce, in southwest Poland, a stork nest is said to be a hundred years old.

---

*   Kubica, *Extermination at KL Auschwitz of Poles*, 244.

———

Czesława scratches herself all the time. She scratches her arms, her legs, raw. She is covered with flea bites, with lice.

"Try not to scratch," Katarzyna, whose body is also covered with bites and sores, tells Czesława. "It makes things worse. You, too, Krystyna, listen to me. Don't scratch."

"Too bad Dama——" Czesława starts to say but does not finish.

Dama is the cow whose urine she had collected in a bucket to cure her rash. A Polish Red cow, Dama is sturdy, dual-purpose—beef and milk—and adaptive. She is brown.

The resettled Germans who took over the Polish farms were not farmers. They did not know how to sow, plow, feed the pigs and chickens, or how to milk a cow. One of them also left a pasture gate open. Her udders heavy with milk, Dama wandered off. No one paid attention to her. A soldier on patrol did. He aimed his machine gun at her but did not shoot. Instead, he shouted something that made the other soldiers laugh—*du blöde Kuh*—the stupid cow. Oblivious, Dama trotted off.

From Wólka Złojecka, Dama trotted for hours in the rain until she reached the Roztocze Forest. Along the way several people tried to catch her. A boy threw a stone at her but missed, a woman yelled and waved what looked like a sheet at her, a man ran after her holding a stick, but Dama did not stop. She had good instincts. Once in the Roztocze Forest, a young woman with untidy long hair milked her, then half a dozen men in ragged clothing, who spoke in a language she recognized, emerged from behind the trees and greedily drank her milk.

"*Piękna krowa*—beautiful cow," one of the men told Dama, patting her thick brown neck.

The estate in Zwierzyniec where both Jan Tomasz Zamoyski and his wife live (and where the Germans have set up another internment camp for the Zamość region) is on the edge of the Roztocze Forest, a forest that Jan Tomasz Zamoyski knows well.

"We are fortunate not to have been deported like the others and that I am allowed to administer the estate," Jan Tomasz Zamoyski repeatedly tells his wife, Róża. "We are also fortunate to live close to the forest. I love the forest. I know the forest like the back of my hand," he adds.

"I know. So you've said," Róża says with a smile.

"And how many times have we ridden our horses through those woods and fields?" Jan Tomasz Zamoyski asks his wife with a sigh.

The horses, regrettably, are gone—beautiful half-Arab, half-thoroughbred beasts—appropriated by the Germans, who ride them too hard.

Róża Zamoyska has gotten used to missing those horses. She has gotten used to missing her life of leisure, privilege, and travel. Only occasionally does she think about the happy time she had during her honeymoon driving with her husband along the Amalfi coast and staying at luxurious cliffside hotels with breathtaking views of the dark blue Tyrrhenian Sea.

But she does miss her father terribly.

Andrzej Zółtowski, Róża's father, was arrested by the Gestapo for refusing to disclose the whereabouts of two of the employees on his estate who were active in the underground, and he died at Auschwitz in September 1941.[*]

At night and on foot, Jan Tomasz Zamoyski, a member of the Home Army, risks his life to supply food and weapons to the partisans hiding in the forest. The Home Army is the largest Polish resistance organization loyal to the Polish government in exile in London. By the war's end, the Home Army has more than 200,000 members and by then, too, Jan Tomasz Zamoyski has been made a colonel.

Ignacy Jan Paderewski, the Polish pianist and composer, was the head of the National Council of Poland, the Polish government in exile in London.

"Ah, Paderewski," Jan Tomasz Zamoyski exclaims, recalling him fondly. He also likes to tell how, before the war, when he and his family were living in Paris, Paderewski would come

[*]   Kubica, *Extermination at KL Auschwitz of Poles*, 260n8.

and dine with them and how, afterward, he played for them on their grand Erard piano.

"An Erard piano is famous for introducing the double escapement lever that allows the pianist to repeat a note quickly," Jan Tomasz explains. "At the time, I was very interested in music and when I told Paderewski that I wanted to be a composer, he encouraged me and I enrolled at a music conservatory. Of course, my father, who was the minister of foreign affairs of Poland, was not pleased. 'Do you want to end up a busker?' he told me." Jan Tomasz gave a laugh.

"Growing up, I rarely saw my father as he was occupied with his government duties," Jan Tomasz continues to reminisce. "In fact, my younger brother, Marek, never saw him at all. And one day—this story always makes me laugh— Marek saw a beautifully dressed doorman, working in one of the hotels in Paris, who was wearing a red coat with gold buttons and gold epaulettes, and Marek cried out, 'That must be my father!' and ran over and embraced the man. The man was very surprised."[*]

Every morning on her way to work, to clear the pond, and every evening on her way back from gathering the silt and pushing the heavy wheelbarrow up the embankment, Krystyna nods toward a group of men whom she sees on

---

[*] "Ordynat. Jan Zamoyski," Sandek 17, June 15, 2021, YouTube, https://www.youtube.com/watch?v=enHqKCxTWCw.

the other side of the electric fence and says the same thing to Czesława.

"I see my father."

Huddled together in their striped blue-and-gray uniforms, the men are too far away for Krystyna to recognize any of them. And they all look alike—dirty, thin, exhausted, nearly dead.

"I am going to wave to him," Krystyna continues.

"Don't," Czesława tells her.

"My father is standing over there," Krystyna says again. "I would know my *tata* anywhere."

Julian Trześniewski, aged 37, died at Auschwitz on February 19, 1943.

During the war, 750,000 Germans were resettled into the area of Poland that had been taken over by the Reich, while 400,000 Poles from that same area were resettled elsewhere. Another 300,000 Poles were shot.

While in the Zamość camp, Krystyna's mother, Katarzyna Trześniewski, gave birth to a baby who died. Soon after, Katarzyna was deported with her three small children to the town of Siedlce. In Siedlce, her children were taken away and sent to other families in other towns.

A badly tattered photo shows Ryszard Trześniewski, aged three, walking hand in hand with an older couple—

the couple who took him in after he was separated from his mother.[*]

After liberation, of the 480 children that Róża Zamoyska was able to save from the Zwierzyniec camp, a third were returned to a parent or to a relative who had managed to survive.

Two photos taken before the war show Róża with her dogs— dogs that look like spaniels. In one photo she is holding a bunch of puppies on her lap; in the other she is sitting on the ground surrounded by three dogs and she is laughing.[†]

"If Kala, my cat, was here, she would get rid of all the rats," Krystyna tells Czesława. "Kala was a great hunter."

"If Kinga, my hen, was here, we would have plenty of eggs," Czesława answers.

"Her eggs were a lovely pale blue," she also says.

Czesława remembers how each time she went in to feed the chickens the rooster would fly at her. It got so she had to take a broom or a rake into the chicken coop to defend herself.

"I hated the rooster," she tells Krystyna. "He was always trying to attack me. He attacked my father, too, and my father threatened to wring the rooster's neck."

---

[*]   Kubica, *Extermination at KL Auschwitz of Poles*, 124.

[†]   Ewa, "40 rocznica śmierci Róży Zamoyskiej—patronki Kola Przewodników w Zamościu," Prewodnicy w Zamościu, October 15, 2016, http:// przewodnicyzamosc.pl/archiwa/4462, accessed December 20, 2023.

Again, Krystyna tells Czesława how much she misses her father and how, for her thirteenth birthday, he made her a beautiful pair of red leather shoes.

"I wish I had those shoes," she says.

Czesława says nothing. She is wearing the dead woman's shoes.

"Every day," Rudolf Höss, the camp commander, proudly told Heinrich Himmler, "at least twenty boxcars filled with the prisoners' confiscated property are loaded on to the Auschwitz railroad ramp."

The damaged or unusable clothes were sent to the Reich Ministry of Economy for industrial processing; the reusable bed linen, towels, blankets were sent to VoMi (Coordination Center for Ethnic Germans) to be given to the German settlers; the remaining clothes and shoes were sent to other concentration camps.[*]

"My wife, Hedwig, found a nice purse among those goods. A French leather purse," Höss tells Himmler. "It was barely used," he adds.

Rudolf Höss found himself a barely used fourteen-year-old girl from Zkierbieszów. Salomea Węcławik was a virgin.

On arrival at Auschwitz, the prisoners judged unfit for work are taken to the crematorium yard, where they are told that

---

[*]   Gutman and Berenbaum, *Anatomy of the Auschwitz Death Camp*, 25.

they have to undergo disinfection—delousing and bathing. They are brought into a dressing room where there are benches and hooks with numbers for their clothes (the prisoners are told to remember the numbers so that they can retrieve their clothes after their bath). After undressing—men and women are separated unless there is not enough time—they are given a piece of soap and a towel and are led to the gas chamber. On their way, they can see signs: "To the Baths." The signs are written in several languages. Once they are inside the gas chamber, the doors are bolted and locked and the Zyklon B pellets are poured into the vents leading into the chamber. It takes no more than twenty minutes for all the prisoners inside to die.*

The narrator in Tadeusz Borowski's story "This Way for the Gas, Ladies and Gentlemen" watches as a trainload of prisoners arrive at Auschwitz, oblivious to their fate and to that of their belongings:

> *They do not know that in just a few moments they will die, that the gold, money, and diamonds which they have so prudently hidden in their clothing and on their bodies are now useless to them. Experienced professionals will probe into every recess of their flesh, will pull the gold from under*

---

* Gutman and Berenbaum, *Anatomy of the Auschwitz Death Camp,* 169–70, 173.

the tongue and the diamonds from the uterus and the colon.
They will rip out gold teeth. In tightly sealed crates they
*will ship them to Berlin.**

"My hair was blond," Czesława tells Krystyna. "A golden blond, my mother called it. It came down to nearly my waist. Sometimes I wore my hair in a braid, a single braid," she continues. "And for holidays—for Easter, for instance—my mother would braid it in a special way." With her hands, she shows Krystyna how her mother would gather individual strands of hair and blend them into larger strands.

Besides her woolen coat, the light blue cotton dress with the yellow zigzag pattern that was missing a few buttons, her underwear, her shoes and socks, and the jacks and rubber ball that she had kept in the coat pocket, Czesława misses her long hair.

"Now, my hair has gotten all dark and ugly," Czesława also says, touching her shorn head.

The thread spun from the prisoners' hair was used to make yarn, felt, and socks for submarine crews and for railroad workers. One kilo (2.2 pounds) of hair was worth 0.50 Reichsmark—about $1.09. By 1943, the twenty boxcars filled daily with the prisoners' confiscated property, which

---

* Borowski, "This Way for the Gas, Ladies and Gentlemen," 48–49.

Rudolf Höss boasted about to Himmler, also held sacks of human hair.[*]

One night in February, a woman from Czesława's barrack tried to escape by throwing a blanket over the electric barbed-wire fence. She was electrocuted anyway.

"It was during the eclipse of the moon," Czesława's mother, Katarzyna, tells the others. "She thought she could get away without being seen."

"An eclipse?" Czesława asks.

"An eclipse occurs when the Earth comes between the moon and the sun," Katarzyna tells Czesława. "You must have learned that in school."

When the Germans invaded Poland, they shut down all the schools and universities.

Czesława's primary school—grades 1 through 8—was in the village of Sitaniec.

Her favorite subject was geography.

"The woman who was electrocuted with the blanket was from Hungary," Katarzyna says.

More than forty women tried to escape from Auschwitz, most of them failed. When the women were caught, they

---

[*]   Gutman and Berenbaum, *Anatomy of the Auschwitz Death Camp*, 259–60.

were publicly hanged, or, if shot while escaping, their corpses were hung and left there for days for the prisoners to see.

Czesława rarely thinks about Pawel, her father. His quick, hot temper frightens her. Pawel is always ready to criticize her, to threaten her, to beat her, and she makes a point of keeping out of his way.

"Little whore! Where have you been?" Pawel calls out to her the day Anton makes her walk the rest of the way home on foot and she is late feeding the chickens.

Then Pawel slaps her hard across the face.

The *kapo* who hit Czesława as she lined up to be photographed is a Pole. Like many of the other prisoner functionaries at Auschwitz, Wacek Ruski is a hardened criminal and known for his brutality. His favorite method of punishing a prisoner is to throw the prisoner to the ground then press the handle of a shovel on his neck and stand on it.

As was her habit, Czesława had opened her mouth to drink in the snow when Ruski hit her, knocking her down.

Czesława is thin. Her hip bones stick out, sharp as knives. Her legs and arms are sticks. Katarzyna, her mother, too, is thin, as is Krystyna. In their bunk, at night, their three bodies pressed together are just brittle bones.

Although she does not speak of it, Czesława still thinks about Anton. Anton will arrive in his plane and fly away with her.

"Where do you want to go?" he asks.

"I want to go where I can see elephants," Czesława replies. "I want to see camels and giraffes."

Stanislaw Skalski, the top Polish fighter pilot, was credited with shooting down 18½ German planes—he claimed to have shot down 22—and was the first Pole to command an RAF squadron. His many awards include: the Golden Cross, the Silver Cross, the Cross of Valour (four times), Poland's Cross of Grunwald, the Distinguished Service Order, and the British Distinguished Flying Cross.

Polish pilots Witold Urbanowicz, Jan Zumbach, Miroslaw Feric, and Zdzislaw Henneberg also received the British Distinguished Flying Cross.

The Allies claimed that the reason they did not bomb Auschwitz was that they got the information about the extermination camps too late. They claimed that military operations should not be conducted for civilian purposes, especially since air power would be more effective on other fronts.

Although Marianna Rycaj knows about the medicinal property of herbs and plants, she can do little for the women in her barrack who are suffering from combinations of frostbite, pneumonia, pleurisy, ulcers, abscesses, typhus, malnutrition, dysentery, and diarrhea. They all have diarrhea.

Diarrhea, diarrhea, diarrhea.

In the diary he wrote while awaiting his trial, Rudolf Höss, the commander of Auschwitz, acknowledged the squalid conditions of the women's barracks:

> They were far more tightly packed in, and the sanitary and hygienic conditions were notably inferior. Furthermore the disastrous overcrowding and its consequences, which existed from the very beginning, prevented any proper order being established in the women's camp.
>
> The general congestion was far greater than in the men's camp. When the women had reached the bottom, they would let themselves go completely. They would then stumble about like ghosts, without any will of their own, and had to be pushed everywhere by the others, until the day came when they quietly passed away. Those stumbling corpses were a terrible sight.[*]

Marianna Rycaj is gassed on July 8, 1943.

"Tell us more about Kraków," Marianna Rycaj says to Katarzyna. "I've never been.

---

[*] Hoess, *Commandant of Auschwitz*, 134–35.

"But my son, Mieczyslaw, went to Kraków with his school," Marianna also says. "What he said he remembered best was the Iron Knife that hangs from the ceiling in the Cloth Tower. Typical of a boy to remember that." Marianna Rycaj gives a little laugh. "He said the knife was used to cut off the ears of criminals."

The women are sitting on their bunks eating their supper of stale bread and moldy cheese.

Again, Czesława is tempted to tell Marianna about how Mieczyslaw used to tease their dog. Instead, she says to her mother, "And tell about the two brothers."

"A long time ago, during the reign of Bolesław Wstydliwy," Katarzyna begins in a slow low voice, "two brothers were commissioned to build the towers of the Church of St. Mary's—the church stands across from the Cloth Tower in Kraków's main square. It's a beautiful church. I wish you could see it," Katarzyna says with a sigh. "The brothers each built a tower and it turned out that one tower was much taller than the other—you can see the difference to this day—and it looks very odd."

Shutting her eyes, Katarzyna is silent.

"Go on," Czesława urges her mother. "Tell what happened."

"When the brother who built the shorter tower discovers this—he is the younger brother—" Katarzyna continues, "he is so jealous and angry that he kills his older brother, who built the taller tower. But, later, when the church was consecrated, the younger brother feels such remorse and guilt for murdering his brother that he stabs himself with a knife—the same knife with which he killed his brother—then he falls dead from the roof of the tower he built."

"He used the Iron Knife that hangs in the Cloth Hall," Czesława says. She has heard the story before. Then she says, "I forget. What were the brothers' names?"

Closing her eyes again, Katarzyna does not answer. She is exhausted from talking.

Mieczyslaw and Tadeusz.

Czesława conflates the two brothers who built the towers with the two boys killed with phenol injections to the heart.

In the winter of 1942 two large crematoriums were built in Auschwitz and were operational in the spring of 1943. Those crematoriums consisted of five three-retort ovens and had the capacity to cremate 2000 people in twenty-four hours. The changing rooms and gas chambers were located underground and the bodies were taken up to the ovens in an elevator. A wall of hedges was to be built to keep the crematoriums out of sight but the hedges were never planted.*

Often, if the crematoriums were full or malfunctioning, naked corpses of the dead piled one on top of the other lay outside.

---

* Hoess, *Commandant at Auschwitz*, 191–92.

———

"Don't look," Katarzyna warns Czesława on their way to work.

Czesława looks.

"Where Auschwitz stands today, three years ago there were villages and farms" is how the Polish writer and Auschwitz survivor Tadeusz Borowski describes the town in a short story. *"There were rich meadows, shaded country lanes, apple orchards. There were people, no better nor worse than any other people."**

Czesława will never read Tadeusz Borowski.

Jan Tomasz Zamoyski and his wife, Róża, may have read Tadeusz Borowski although, again, they may not have. They may have wanted to forget and to put the awful past behind them. They may—however impossible—have wanted to try to live their lives as before.

A "paradise of flowers" is how Hedwig, Rudolf Höss's wife, describes her garden at Auschwitz. "Especially my beautiful roses!" she gushes. "Red roses that come all the way from Germany—from Steinfurth." Hedwig Höss also claims to be very fond of her two gardeners, who are prisoners. "I forget their names but no matter. I call them Max and Moritz,

---

* Borowski, "Auschwitz, Our Home (A Letter)," 132.

after the naughty boys in the children's book," she says with a laugh, "and my daughters, Inge-Brigitt and Heidetraud, give Max and Moritz special treats."

The whole Höss family loves nature and animals—horses and dogs, and, especially, the little dachshund Schatzie.

The red poppy, also known as the corn poppy, is Poland's national flower. It blooms in the rich black soil of Pawel's wheat fields.

"Don't bother to pick the poppies," Katarzyna tells Czesława. "The petals fall off right away and the flowers don't last."

For special occasions and for feast days, Katarzyna bakes bread with poppy seeds.

The thought of the bread makes Czesława weep.

"Have you ever had a *karpatka*?" Czesława asks Krystyna.

"Don't talk to me about food," Krystyna answers.

Czesława and Krystyna no longer have the strength or desire to play jacks.

Pushing the heavy wheelbarrow full of silt up the steep embankment, Czesława slips and, yelling, a guard sets a dog on her. As Czesława struggles to stand, the dog lunges at her, knocks her to the ground again, and bites her.

The guard laughs.

"It's a dog. No, you've no business here. Off you go . . ."

In *Kaytek the Wizard*, the book Czesława has read and reread, Kaytek is punished for his lack of humility and turned into a dog. When he goes home, his parents do not recognize him.

> *"Father, Daddy," Kaytek whimpers*
> *"Maybe he's hungry," Kaytek's mother says.*
> *But Kaytek does not want food. He's only hungry for a kind word, for his parents' caress.*
> *"If you don't want food, be off with you, before I lose my patience."*
> *Kaytek jumps up, leans his paws against his father's chest and stares him in the eye.*
> *"Get lost!"**

"Dogs aren't naturally vicious," Czesława tells Krystyna.

"I don't like dogs," Krystyna says. "I like cats."

"I saw my *tata*, again, today. He waved to me," feverish, Krystyna insists.

Czesława does not answer. Her leg hurts. The calf is nearly fleshless and the dog bit into the bone.

Perhaps, she thinks, the dog that bit her is really a boy.

What had the guard called him? Hansi?

Hans. A tall blond German boy, punished for his sins.

---

* Korczak, *Kaytek the Wizard*, 247, 249.

————

According to the treaty signed by the Soviets that granted amnesty to the 300,000 Poles deported to Russia, the 110,000, who had managed to survive the ordeal, were making their painful and slow way from Siberia to Iran, first on foot, then by train. Anton is one of them.

Considering himself fortunate, Anton manages to get on a train crowded with refugees at Nizhny Novgorod. A Russian industrial city, Nizhny Novgorod is the largest supplier of military equipment for the war and the objective of Germany's frequent aerial attacks. During the night while Anton sleeps, a group of Luftwaffe planes fly over the Somovo Iron Works which is next to the railway station. Several incendiary bombs destroy the station, the train, and kill Anton. The iron works is only lightly damaged.

The Polish Air Force flew a total of 102,486 sorties, lost 1973 men and shot down 745 German planes and 190 V-1 rockets.[*]

A loud whistle wakes Czesława. A guard is shouting, pushing, shoving. Everyone has to get out of the bunks. Those who are slow are beaten. A roll call. The women are made to stand in rows outside in the cold. It is early in the morning

[*]   Adam Zamoyski, *Poland: A History* (New York: Hippocrene, 2012), 320.

and still dark. Like the other women, Czesława is wearing only her striped uniform and wooden clogs. It is windy and it has begun to sleet. For several hours, they must not move or speak.

A few of the women from the Zamość region who will freeze to death that day or die soon after are:

KATARZYNA KWOKA—prisoner number 26946

ANIELA BELINA—prisoner number 26823

MARIANNA RYCAJ—prisoner number 27038

KATARZYNA SUDAK—prisoner number 27046

ELŻBIETA SAŁAMACHA—prisoner number 27055

STEFANIA SZABAT—prisoner number 27056

KAROLINA SAŁAMACHA—prisoner number 27057

FRANCISZKA KAPLON—prisoner number 26915

STEFANIA PIRÓG—number 27022

AGNIESZKA FLACZ—prisoner number 26864

WANDA WRÓBEL—prisoner number 27100

ANNA PROC—prisoner number 27019

ANNA PUZIO—prisoner number 27010

All but Feliksa Rycyk. She is one of the few women from the Zamość region to have survived Auschwitz. Evacuated to Bergen-Belsen, she was liberated in 1945.[*]

---

[*]   Kubica, *Extermination at KL Auschwitz of Poles*, 54.

———

As for Stefania Szabat, who must have slipped in between the two sisters, Elżbieta and Karolina Sałamacha, as they waited in line to be tattooed, nothing about her, except her age—twenty-six—has been recorded. Not even the date of her death. Stefania must have been one of the remaining 4000 Jews from the Zamość Ghetto—her surname, Szabat, is from the Hebrew *shabbat* meaning Sabbath—who, on October 11, 1942, managed to avoid being sent to the Bełżec death camp and, instead, a few months later, was sent to Auschwitz.

The guard in charge of the early morning roll call is from Rudelsdorf, a small town in Bavaria. His name is Adolf Taube and he is a member of the Waffen-SS. He is tall, dark-haired, and in his mid-thirties. Each time he selects a delinquent or sick woman prisoner for the gas chamber he lets out a triumphant yodel—*Ay-ee-ay-ee-ooo.*

Franciszka Kaplon is one of the women who can no longer stand outside in the cold and kneels, then she lets herself fall to the ground.

Ay-ee-ay-ee-ooo.

According to the deposition of a Czech Auschwitz survivor at the Bergen-Belsen war crimes trial, conducted by the British, Adolf Taube, who was in charge of Block 25, known as the Death Block, was an exceptionally cruel guard. He specialized in lengthy roll calls and took pleasure in beating women prisoners and shooting them at random and for sport.

A woman who is standing next to Franciszka Kaplon begins to wail and Adolf Taube shoots her in the stomach.

Ay-ee-ay-ee-ooo.

And although criminal charges were brought against hundreds of SS men and women from the Auschwitz camp after the war—the trial and execution of Rudolf Höss, the camp commander, is the most notorious example—Adolf Taube was not among those tried nor was he ever held accountable.

"Where is Stefania Szabat from? What village, do you know?" Karolina Sałamacha asks her sister. She and Elżbieta are from the village of Sitaniec.

(Karolina did not see Czesława ride to and from Zamość on the back of Anton's motorcycle, but, from the kitchen of her house, she did hear the roar of a motorcycle on that day and remembers complaining about the noise to her sister.)

"I don't know. I did not dare speak to her otherwise a guard would have beaten me," Elżbieta Sałamacha replies.

"She should not have pushed herself in line between us," still resentful, Karolina continues.

"I felt sorry for her. She was without relatives and as soon as she got her tattoo, I saw them take her away," Elżbieta says.

"Who knows where," Karolina also says. "She was young and quite pretty."

"Block 10," Elżbieta predicts.

Elżbieta Sałamacha, aged 39, is gassed on February 25, 1943.

Karolina Sałamacha, aged 30, is gassed nine days later, on March 6, 1943.

Block 10 is the site of the most horrific medical experiments. Many of the experiments deal with the sterilization of women.

Block 10 also houses about twenty prostitutes, young women who are offered a bit more bread and better living conditions. The women are sterilized and only the missionary position is allowed; fifteen minutes is allotted to the act—SS guards watch through spy holes to make sure these rules are followed—race laws are enforced and Germans can couple with Germans, Slavs with Slavs. Jews and Russians are forbidden.*

The infection has spread and when Czesława shows her leg to her mother, Katarzyna says that, perhaps, Czesława should go see a doctor in the hospital. Then, again, Katarzyna right

* Gutman and Berenbaum; *Anatomy of the Auschwitz Death Camp*, 304, 306.

away says, no, perhaps she should not. They have heard enough horror stories about the hospital.

"Perhaps, the bite will heal by itself," Katarzyna says without conviction.

When Czesława shows her dog bite to Marianna Rycaj, Marianna prods the skin around the wound and asks, "Can you feel this?"

Czesława is barely listening. She wants to lie down and sleep.

"But don't go to the hospital," Marianna tells her.

"You should go to the hospital," Krystyna tells Czesława.

Dr. Eduard Wirths's methods—although he rarely operates on the prisoners himself—are either to remove the woman's ovaries surgically or to sterilize the ovaries with radiation. Other experiments consist of injecting a woman's cervix with a caustic substance—probably formalin.

"Do you want to play jacks?" Krystyna asks Czesława, to take her mind off her leg.

Czesława shakes her head.

"Marianna Rycaj is right. If you go to the hospital, they may amputate your leg," Krystyna tells her.

"My grandfather had a wooden leg. He was shot in the war. The First World War. He got used to it and hardly limped. My father made him a special shoe for his wooden leg."

Lying on the filthy straw in the bunk, Czesława is asleep.

"Are you going to eat your soup?" Krystyna asks. "Or can I have it?"

If, on her arrival at Auschwitz, Stefania Szabat is unlucky, she is sent to Block 10; if she is lucky, she is sent to the gas chamber.

Rudolf Höss, the commandant of Auschwitz, holds Dr. Eduard Wirths, Auschwitz's chief medical officer, in high regard. Comparing Dr. Wirths with the other doctors, Höss was quoted as saying: "During my ten years of service in concentration camp affairs, I have never encountered a better one."*

Hedwig, Höss's wife, is equally enthusiastic about Gertrud, Dr. Wirths's wife.

"I like her children, too," she tells her husband.

"Gertrud came for lunch today. We had *schweinbraten* and dumplings," Hedwig continues. "The children played together in the garden and Gertrud got to admire my roses. Poor Gertrud. She complained that she misses her family in Bavaria. To cheer her up, I showed her my new purse," Hed-

---

* Robert Jay Lifton, *The Nazi Doctors: Medical Killing and the Psychology of Genocide* (New York: Basic Books, 1986), 386.

wig says, laughing, "and I told her she should go and have a look. She might find something she likes there among all those discarded Jewish goods."

"What did you have for dessert?" Rudolf Höss asks his wife. He has a sweet tooth.

"A fruit compote," Hedwig answers. "With fresh cream," she adds.

Rudolf Höss smacks his lips.

"I'll show you how. It's easy," Katarzyna told Czesława about making butter.

School closed, Czesława is home all day and she has to take turns with her mother at the wooden churn.

The repetitive movement is tedious and Czesława's arms ache. If the weather is too hot the butter comes out soft, if too cold, the butter does not stick together.

"It will do you good," Katarzyna had also told Czesława. "It will teach you patience."

Eduard Wirths left a collection of photographs showing the construction of the hospital at Auschwitz and showing prisoners digging holes for the foundation. In one photo, two nurses are seen from the back bicycling down a road.

Nearly every day on her way back from work clearing the pond of mud, Czesława sees a woman riding away on her bicycle. Some days the woman bicycles with another woman, other days she bicycles alone. Czesława does not know who she is but, from her uniform, she can tell that the woman is a nurse. The woman bicycles fast, expertly avoiding potholes in the road.

"My *tata* taught me how to ride a bicycle," Krystyna tells Czesława.

"You had a bicycle?" Czesława does not always believe everything Krystyna says.

"A bicycle with a basket," Krystyna lies.

"Maria is a good nurse," Wirths tells his wife, Gertrud, about one of the cyclists, "but, at times, she tends to be too kind to the patients. Just this morning, I caught her feeding one of them—a toothless young woman. More than once," he continues, "I had to remind Maria that the prisoners are our enemies."

"I admire her courage," Gertrud murmurs.

When in September 1945, he was captured by the Allies and held by the British forces, and knowing he would have to face trial, Eduard Wirths hung himself.

In a letter to her sister about volunteering to go and work at Auschwitz, Maria Stromberger, an Austrian Red Cross nurse, wrote, "I want to see how things really are; perhaps I can do some good there."

As head nurse at the SS hospital and, at the risk of her own life, she tried to help prisoners by giving them extra food and smuggling letters and packages for them.[*]

After the war, Maria Stromberger testified at the Nuremberg trials against Rudolf Höss.

"The women in No. [Block] 10 are being artificially inseminated, injected with typhoid and malaria germs, or operated on," writes Tadeusz Borowski—chosen out of thousands of inmates to be a medical orderly—in another of his short stories, which takes the form of a letter. *"The women are kept behind barred and boarded-up windows, but still the place is often broken into and the women are inseminated, not at all artificially."*[†]

Although liberated from Auschwitz at the end of the war and able to return to his home in Warsaw, marry his fiancée, father a little girl, Tadeusz Borowski turned on the gas in his apartment and killed himself on July 1, 1951. He was twenty-nine years old.

The spread of bacteria from infected lice, fleas, and rats in the block's crowded living conditions causes typhus. Fever, head-

---

[*] Elizabeth Hanink, "Maria Stromberger (1898–1957)—Austrian Nurse Who Risked Her Life to Aid Auschwitz Prisoners," *Working Nurse*, March 12, 2018, https://www.workingnurse.com/articles/maria-stromberger-1898-1957-austrian-nurse-who-risked-her-life-to-aid-auschwitz-prisoners/, accessed December 22, 2023.

[†] Borowski, "Auschwitz, Our Home (A Letter)," 108.

aches, muscle aches, coughing, nausea, vomiting, and a rash are among the symptoms of typhus.

The women also suffer from dysentery, typhoid, measles, tuberculosis, malnutrition, exhaustion, and injuries from beatings.

At the slightest provocation, Pawel, Czesława's father, beats her. He beats Czesława with whatever is closest at hand—a broom, a stick, or just with the back of his hand—while Katarzyna, her mother, has never hit or slapped Czesława. Instead, Katarzyna treats Czesława with brusqueness and stoicism.

"Stop complaining," she tells Czesława. "A bee sting is nothing. I'll put some vinegar on it. Go now and shell the peas so I won't be late with dinner."

Only on occasions when Katarzyna can leave off her cooking, cleaning, washing, milking, does her manner soften, and she asks Czesława, "Have I told you about how when I was a girl your age in Kraków I wanted to become a teacher. . . ."

Czesława has not yet made up her mind what she would like to be. For a while, she wished she could be a boy—have the freedom boys have.

If only she could kiss her elbow! An impossible feat and an old wives' tale that her *babciu* believed could result in a sex change.

Now she is not so sure.

A nurse, perhaps.

———

At the end of the war, the Soviets confiscated all of Jan Tomasz Zamoyski's properties and, along with his younger brother Marek, arrested him. Jan Tomasz Zamoyski languished in a prison cell in the city of Kielce for eight months without a trial, until he and his brother were released. Then in 1949, Jan Tomasz was again arrested on trumped-up charges of espionage, and, after a two-year investigation, sentenced to twenty-five years in prison. He was sent to Rakowiecka prison in Warsaw, where he was tortured, then to a labor camp in Piechcin, until he was released from prison in 1956.

While her husband was in prison, Róża Zamoyska—forced into semi-exile and living in a rented house on the outskirts of Warsaw—worked as a professional nurse to provide for their children.

Clearly, Róża Zamoyska loved her husband very much. On their wedding anniversary, since they were not together at the time, she wrote to him: *Darling, being far away that day, I think we were able to keep the prescription of our common love, let it last and in this spirit I write, my only one.*[*]

Katarzyna's emaciated body is covered with a red rash. She vomits up her ration of stale bread and rotted vegetable soup.

[*] "Listopadowe Zwiedzanie Zamościa—Katedra, Rotunda, Miej-sca Pamięci," Przewodnik po Zamościu i Roztoczu, https://przewodnikzamosc.pl/?tag=roza-zamoyska, accessed December 22, 2023.

She rarely thinks of Tomasz—only occasionally in a flash of memory—Tomasz running across the airfield, Tomasz swinging his leather helmet, Tomasz smiling, Tomasz's lips on hers. . . .

Katarzyna has lost her teeth.

Katarzyna of the red dress is unrecognizable.

Katarzyna Kwoka, age 47, dies on February 18, 1943.

> FRANCISZKA KAPLON, age 38, is the first among the group of women from the villages of Sitaniec and Wólka Złojecka to die, on January 1, 1943
>
> Both ANNA PROC, age 53, and ANNA PUZIO, age 55, die on February 6, 1943
>
> ANIELA BELINA, age 45, dies on February 20, 1943, two days after Katarzyna Kwoka
>
> STEFANIA PIRÓG dies on February 25, 1943, five days after Aniela Belina
>
> ELŻBIETA SAŁAMACHA, age 39, dies on February 25, 1943, the same day as Aniela Belina
>
> Her sister, KAROLINA SAŁAMACHA, age 30, dies on March 3, 1943
>
> AGNEISZKA FLACZ, age 52, dies on March 16, 1943
>
> KATARZYNA SUDAK, age 47, also dies on March 16, 1943
>
> WANDA WRÓBEL, age 17, dies on July 16, 1943
>
> MARIANNA RYCAJ, AGE 55, is the last woman from the group to die, on July 8, 1943

———

Róża Zamoyska dies in Warsaw on October 15, 1976, in a freak bus accident.

A heartbreak.

Róża did not get to see her husband, Jan Tomasz Zamoyski, become an Honorary Citizen of the city of Janów Lubelski in 1990; nor, that same year, did she see him get elected leader of the National Democratic Party and, a year later, elected senator of Zamość Province; nor, more important—and she would have been so proud and happy—in 1995, receive Poland's highest decoration, the Order of the White Eagle, from Lech Wałęsa; and finally, in 1996, receive the title of Honorary Citizen of the city of Zamość.

Jan Tomasz Zamoyski, the sixteenth and last *ordynat*, died on June 29, 2002.

For days, the corpse of the woman who tried to escape by throwing a blanket over the electrified fence is hung next to Auschwitz's entrance gate.

Arbeit macht frei—Czesława does not know what the German words on the sign mean.

But walking by the corpse twice a day, Czesława cannot help but look.

Dangling from the rope around her neck, the woman looks like a puppet.

She has lost one of her shoes.

The shoe is lying on the ground and when, on the way back to the barrack, one of the prisoners leans down to pick it up, a guard shoots her.

When Czesława was four or five years old, she was taken to a puppet show. She does not remember where—perhaps to the village of Sitaniec. The puppet show was based on Maria Konopnicka's popular children's fairy tale *Little Orphan Mary and the Gnomes*.

"An orphan," Katarzyna explains to Czesława, "is a child who loses her parents."

"Why can't she find them?" Czesława asks.

"Don't worry, the story ends happily. Little Mary is adopted by a nice peasant family."

But the puppets frighten her—especially the puppets of the gnomes with their animal heads—and Czesława starts to cry while the other children laugh.

"Do you know the story of *Little Orphan Mary and the Gnomes*?" Czesława asks Krystyna. For years after the puppet show, she had nightmares about those gnomes.

"Those gnomes frightened me."

"Gnomes are like dwarves. My *tata* once made a pair of shoes—little shoes—for a dwarf and—" Krystyna says, starting to laugh, then starting to cough. Krystyna coughs blood.

Krystyna Trześniewska, age 13, dies on May 18, 1943.

———

Cold, hungry, sick with typhus, and limping from the dog bite on her leg, Czesława has forgotten most things. Only in her dreams does Czesława remember:

> Her lace communion dress muddied on a
>> motorcycle ride past unfamiliar dark trees
>
> Her father twisting the rooster's neck and laughing
> The dead calf struggling to its feet
> Painted eggshells lying scattered on the floor and
>> her mother weeping
>
> Searching all over for her missing shoe and sure to
>> be punished
>
> Anton's plane spiraling down to earth in a ball of
>> fire and the dog barking
>
> Her family's bedsheets blowing in the wind
>> while drying on a line then turning into
>> hanged corpses

Curiously, on March 12, 1943, the day Czesława is put to death, just as it had when she arrived on December 13, 1942, it begins to snow at Auschwitz. Down by the pond, while the guard has his back turned to adjust the collar on one of the dogs, Czesława drops her shovel and lifts her face up to the sky and opens her mouth wide to the flakes.

AUTHOR'S NOTE

A LITTLE MORE THAN A DECADE AGO, I READ AN OBITU-
ary in *The New York Times* of the Polish photographer Wilhelm Brasse, who took over 40,000 pictures of the prisoners
at Auschwitz. Three of the photographs included in the obit-
uary were of Czesława Kwoka, a fourteen-year-old Polish
Catholic girl. I cut out the photos and kept them. A prisoner himself, Brasse also took photographs of Czesława's
mother, Katarzyna Kwoka, of Czesława's thirteen-year-old
friend, Krystyna Trześniewska, and of the 644 men, women,
and children in Czesława's transport, most of whom were
exterminated—a fraction of the 75,000 Catholic Poles and
300,000 Jewish Poles who lost their lives at Auschwitz. Czesława was from Wólka Złojecka, one of the 297 small villages
in the Zamość region in southeast Poland from which 110,00
Catholic and Jewish Poles were evicted between November 1941 and August 1943 by the Germans, who were deter-

mined to repopulate the area with their own. Among those evicted from that region, were 30,000 Jewish and Catholic children, of whom 4500, judged to look Aryan enough, were sent to Germany to be adopted and "germanized." During the German occupation, close to 6 million Poles were killed; 3 million were Jews, an estimated 1.8 to 1.9 million were non-Jews who died in either prison, forced labor, executions, or concentration camps, while the rest were other civilian and military casualties.

This is a work of fiction based on fact. In an attempt to bring to life a young life tragically lost, I have borrowed from Tadeuz Borowski's brutal short story and from Janusz Korczak's inspired children's tale, I have invented a garden filled with roses for Hedwig Höss, the Auschwitz commander's unconscionable wife, and, for Czesława, I imagined a pretty orange hen named Kinga, a creamy *karpatka*, a Bible with a white leather cover and a game of jacks, Anton with the nice laugh, and the snow.

I want to thank my editor, Robert Weil.